Dear Reader,

It is a great pleasure for me to congratulate Silhouette Books on its 20th anniversary. I signed my first book contract with Silhouette in 1980. We go back quite a long way together, and it has been a wonderful association. All of us at Silhouette—authors, editors, artists, copy editors, salesmen, publicists and management—are a team. We work together to produce the books which our readers have so loyally purchased all these years.

Before I started writing for Silhouette Books, I was holding down a full-time job as a newspaper reporter, on call twenty-four hours a day. I did feature material for two other newspapers, as well. At night, I wrote books and hoped that someday, someone would want to publish them. Sure enough, in 1980, Silhouette Books decided that I just might suit them. We entered into a partnership. Since they took me on trust, I worked very hard to earn my place as one of their authors.

Each year meant a new book; often many more than one. I can go through the titles of my books, see my life through the pages of the novels I wrote during those years, and revisit warm and sweet memories of people now dead who meant so much to me when I was young and bright with ambition and dreams of publication.

I have had a wonderful career and a wonderful life. God has blessed me with a loving family, many great friends (Especially you, Ann!), the best editors on earth and a way to contribute something to the world which has given me so much. I hope that my books have helped some of you through bad times in your own lives, just as the authors I collect and love have comforted me during the storms of my own life. I wish you continued success, Silhouette Books, and I hope to remain a part of your family until I die or you get tired of me—whichever comes first. Thank you for giving me a chance to do what I love best in all the world. God bless you.

Love to Silhouette and to my very special readers,

Diana Palmer

Dear Reader,

♪♫"Happy Birthday to us...."♪♫ Exactly twenty years ago this May, Silhouette Romance was born. Since then, we've grown as a company, and as a series that continues to offer the very best in contemporary category romance fiction. The icing on the cake is this month's amazing lineup:

International bestselling author Diana Palmer reprises her SOLDIERS OF FORTUNE miniseries with *Mercenary's Woman*. Sorely missed, Rita Rainville returns to Romance with the delightful story of a *Too Hard To Handle* rancher who turns out to be anything but.... Elizabeth August delivers the dramatic finale to ROYALLY WED. In *A Royal Mission*, rescuing kidnapped missing princess Victoria Rockford was easy for Lance Grayson. But falling in love wasn't part of the plan.

Marie Ferrarella charms us with a *Tall, Strong & Cool Under Fire* hero whose world turns topsy-turvy when an adorable moppet and her enticing mom venture into his fire station.... Julianna Morris's BRIDAL FEVER! rages on when *Hannah Gets a Husband*—her childhood friend who is a new dad. And in *Her Sister's Child*, a woman allies with her enemy. Don't miss this pulse-pounding romance by Lilian Darcy!

In June, we're featuring Dixie Browning and Phyllis Halldorson, and in coming months look for new miniseries from many of your favorite authors. It's an exciting year for Silhouette Books, and we invite you to join the celebration!

Happy reading!

Mary-Theresa Hussey

Mary-Theresa Hussey
Senior Editor

Please address questions and book requests to:
Silhouette Reader Service
U.S.: 3010 Walden Ave., P.O. Box 1325, Buffalo, NY 14269
Canadian: P.O. Box 609, Fort Erie, Ont. L2A 5X3

DIANA PALMER

MERCENARY'S
WOMAN
SOLDIERS OF FORTUNE

Published by Silhouette Books

America's Publisher of Contemporary Romance

For the Habersham Co. (GA) Sheriff's Department, and the Habersham Co. Emergency Medical Service, with thanks.

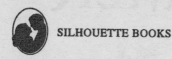 SILHOUETTE BOOKS

ISBN 0-373-19444-7

MERCENARY'S WOMAN

This edition published by arrangement with Harlequin Books S.A.

® and TM are trademarks of Harlequin Books S.A., used under license. Trademarks indicated with ® are registered in the United States Patent and Trademark Office, the Canadian Trade Marks Office and in other countries.

Visit Silhouette at www.eHarlequin.com

Printed in U.S.A.

Books by Diana Palmer

Silhouette Romance

Darling Enemy #254
Roomful of Roses #301
Heart of Ice #314
Passion Flower #328
‡*Soldier of Fortune* #340
After the Music #406
Champagne Girl #436
Unlikely Lover #472
Woman Hater #532
†*Calhoun* #580
†*Justin* #592
†*Tyler* #604
†*Sutton's Way* #670
†*Ethan* #694
†*Connal* #741
†*Harden* #783
†*Evan* #819
†*Donavan* #843
†*Emmett* #910
King's Ransom #971
†*Regan's Pride* #1000
†*Coltrain's Proposal* #1103
Mystery Man #1210
†*The Princess Bride* #1282
†*Callaghan's Bride* #1355
‡*Mercenary's Woman* #1444

Silhouette Books

Silhouette Christmas Stories 1987
"The Humbug Man"

Silhouette Summer Sizzlers 1990
"Miss Greenhorn"

To Mother with Love 1993
"Calamity Mom"

Montana Mavericks
Rogue Stallion

Montana Mavericks Weddings 1998
"The Bride Who Was Stolen in the Night"

Abduction and Seduction 1995
"Redbird"

†*A Long Tall Texan Summer* 1997

Lone Star Christmas 1997
†"Christmas Cowboy"

Love With a Long, Tall Texan 1999

Steeple Hill

Love Inspired
Blind Promises

Silhouette Desire

The Cowboy and the Lady #12
September Morning #26
Friends and Lovers #50
Fire and Ice #80
Snow Kisses #102
Diamond Girl #110
The Rawhide Man #157
Lady Love #175
Cattleman's Choice #193
‡*The Tender Stranger* #230
Love by Proxy #252
Eye of the Tiger #271
Loveplay #289
Rawhide and Lace #306
Rage of Passion #325
Fit for a King #349
Betrayed by Love #391
‡*Enamored* #420
Reluctant Father #469
Hoodwinked #492
His Girl Friday #528
Hunter #606
Nelson's Brand #618
The Best Is Yet To Come #643
*The Case of the Mesmerizing Boss #702
*The Case of the Confirmed Bachelor #715
*The Case of the Missing Secretary #733
Night of Love #799
Secret Agent Man #829
†*That Burke Man* #913
Man of Ice #1000
The Patient Nurse #1099
†*Beloved* #1189

Silhouette Special Edition

Heather's Song #33
The Australian #239
Maggie's Dad #991
†*Matt Caldwell:*
Texas Tycoon #1297

‡ Soldiers of Fortune
† Long, Tall Texans
* Most Wanted Series

IT'S OUR 20th ANNIVERSARY!
We'll be celebrating all year,
Continuing with these fabulous titles,
On sale in May 2000.

Romance

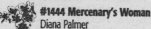

#1444 Mercenary's Woman
Diana Palmer

#1445 Too Hard To Handle
Rita Rainville

#1446 A Royal Mission
Elizabeth August

#1447 Tall, Strong & Cool Under Fire
Marie Ferrarella

 #1448 Hannah Gets a Husband
Julianna Morris

#1449 Her Sister's Child
Lilian Darcy

Desire

 #1291 Dr. Irresistible
Elizabeth Bevarly

 #1292 Expecting His Child
Leanne Banks

#1293 In His Loving Arms
Cindy Gerard

 #1294 Sheikh's Honor
Alexandra Sellers

#1295 The Baby Bonus
Metsy Hingle

#1296 Did You Say Married?!
Kathie DeNosky

Intimate Moments

 #1003 Rogue's Reform
Marilyn Pappano

 #1004 The Cowboy's Hidden Agenda
Kathleen Creighton

#1005 In a Heartbeat
Carla Cassidy

 #1006 Anything for Her Marriage
Karen Templeton

#1007 Every Little Thing
Linda Winstead Jones

 #1008 Remember the Night
Linda Castillo

Special Edition

 #1321 The Kincaid Bride
Jackie Merritt

 #1322 The Millionaire She Married
Christine Rimmer

#1323 Warrior's Embrace
Peggy Webb

 #1324 The Sheik's Arranged Marriage
Susan Mallery

#1325 Sullivan's Child
Gail Link

#1326 Wild Mustang
Jane Toombs

Chapter One

Ebenezer Scott stood beside his double-wheeled black pickup truck and stared openly at the young woman across the street while she fiddled under the hood of a dented, rusted hulk of a vehicle. Sally Johnson's long blond hair was in a ponytail. She was wearing jeans and boots and no hat. He smiled to himself, remembering how many times in the old days he'd chided her about sunstroke. It had been six years since they'd even spoken. She'd been living in Houston until July, when she and her blind aunt and small cousin had moved back, into the decaying old Johnson homestead. He'd seen her several times since her return, but she'd made a point of not speaking to him. He couldn't really blame her. He'd left her with some painful emotional scars.

She was slender, but her trim figure still made his heartbeat jump. He knew how she looked under that loose blouse. His eyes narrowed with heat as he recalled the shocked pleasure in her pale gray eyes when he'd touched her, kissed her, in those forbidden places. He'd meant to frighten her so that she'd stop teasing him, but his impulsive attempt to discourage her had succeeded all too well. She'd run from him then, and she'd kept running. She was twenty-three now, a woman; probably an experienced woman. He mourned for what might have been if she'd been older and he hadn't just come back from leading a company of men into the worst bloodbath of his career. A professional soldier of fortune was no match for a young and very innocent girl. But, then, she hadn't known about his real life—the one behind the facade of cattle ranching. Not many people in this small town did.

It was six years later. She was all grown-up, a schoolteacher here in Jacobsville, Texas. He was…retired, they called it. Actually he was still on the firing line from time to time, but mostly he taught other men in the specialized tactics of covert operations on his ranch. Not that he shared that information. He still had enemies from the old days, and one of them had just been sprung from prison on a technicality—a man out for revenge and with more than enough money to obtain it.

Sally had been almost eighteen the spring day he'd sent her running from him. In a life liberally strewn with regrets, she was his biggest one. The whole situation had been impossible, of course. But he'd never meant to hurt her, and the thought of her sat heavily on his conscience.

He wondered if she knew why he kept to himself and never got involved with the locals. His ranch was a model of sophistication, from its state-of-the-art gym to the small herd of purebred Santa Gertrudis breeding cattle he raised. His men were not only loyal, but tight-lipped. Like another Jacobsville, Texas, resident—Cy Parks—Ebenezer was a recluse. The two men shared more than a taste for privacy. But that was something they kept to themselves.

Meanwhile, Sally Johnson was rapidly losing patience

with her vehicle. He watched her push at a strand of hair that had escaped from the long ponytail. She kept a beef steer or two herself. It must be a frugal existence for her, supporting not only herself, but her recently blinded aunt, and her six-year-old cousin as well.

He admired her sense of responsibility, even as he felt concern for her situation. She had no idea why her aunt had been blinded in the first place, or that the whole family was in a great deal of danger. It was why Jessica had persuaded Sally to give up her first teaching job in Houston in June and come home with her and Stevie to Jacobsville. It was because they'd be near Ebenezer, and Jessica knew he'd protect them. Sally had never been told what Jessica's profession actually was, any more than she knew what Jessica's late husband, Hank Myers, had once done for a living. But even if she had known, wild horses wouldn't have dragged Sally back here if Jessica hadn't pleaded with her, he mused bitterly. Sally had every reason in the world to hate him. But he was her best hope of survival. And she didn't even know it.

In the five months she'd been back in Jacobsville, Sally had managed to avoid Ebenezer. In a town this size, that had been an accomplishment. Inevitably they met from time to time. But Sally avoided eye contact with him. It was the only indication of the painful memory they both shared.

He watched her lean helplessly over the dented fender of the old truck and decided that now was as good a time as any to approach her.

Sally lifted her head just in time to see the tall, lean man in the shepherd's coat and tan Stetson make his way across the street to her. He hadn't changed, she thought bitterly. He still walked with elegance and a slow, arrogance of carriage that seemed somehow foreign. Jeans didn't disguise the muscles in those long, powerful legs as he moved. She hated the ripple of sensation that lifted her heart at his approach. Surely she was over hero worship and infatuation, at her age, especially after what he'd done to her that long-ago spring day. She blushed just remembering it!

He paused at the truck, about an arm's length away from her, pushed his Stetson back over his thick blond-streaked brown hair and impaled her with green eyes.

She was immediately hostile and it showed in the tautening of her features as she looked up, way up, at him.

He raised an eyebrow and studied her flushed face. "Don't give me the evil eye," he said. "I'd have thought you had sense enough not to buy a truck from Turkey Sanders."

"He's my cousin," she reminded him.

"He's the Black Plague with car keys," he countered. "The Hart boys wiped the floor with him not too many years back. He sold Corrigan Hart's future wife a car that fell apart when she drove it off the lot. She was lucky at that," he added with a wicked grin. "He sold old lady Bates a car and told her the engine was optional equipment."

She laughed in spite of herself. "It's not a bad old truck," she countered. "It just needs a few things…"

He glanced at the rear tire and nodded. "Yes. An overhauled engine, a paint job, reupholstered seats, a tailgate that works. And a rear tire that isn't bald." He pointed toward it. "Get that replaced," he said shortly. "You can afford a tire even on what you make teaching."

She gaped at him. "Listen here, Mr. Scott…" she began haughtily.

"You know my name, Sally," he said bluntly, and his eyes were steady, intimidating. "As for the tire, it isn't a request,'' he replied flatly, staring her down. "You've got some new neighbors out your way that I don't like the look of. You can't afford a breakdown in the middle of the night on that lonely stretch of road.''

She drew herself up to her full height, so that the top of her head came to his chin. He really was ridiculously tall...

"This is the twenty-first century, and women are capable of looking after themselves....'' she said heatedly.

"I can do without a current events lecture,'' he cut her off again, moving to peer under the hood. He propped one enormous booted foot on the fender and studied the engine, frowned, pulled out a pocketknife and went to work.

"It's *my* truck!" she fumed, throwing up her hands in exasperation.

"It's half a ton of metal without an engine that works.''

She grimaced. She hated not being able to fix it herself, to have to depend on this man, of all people, for help. She wouldn't let herself think about the cost of having a mechanic make a road service call to get the stupid thing started. Looking at his lean, capable hands brought back painful memories as well. She knew the tenderness of them on concealed skin, and her whole body erupted with sensation.

Less than two minutes later, he repocketed his knife. "Try it now," he said.

She got in behind the wheel. The engine turned noisily, pouring black smoke out of the tailpipe.

He paused beside the open window of the truck, his pale green eyes piercing her face. "Bad rings and valves," he pointed out. "Maybe an oil leak. Either way, you're in for some major repairs. Next time, don't buy from Turkey Sanders, and I don't give a damn if he is a relative.''

"Don't you give me orders," she said haughtily.

That eyebrow lifted again. "Habit. How's Jess?"

She frowned. "Do you know my aunt Jessie?"

"Quite well," he said. "I knew your uncle Hank. He and I served together."

"In the military?"

He didn't answer her. "Do you have a gun?"

She was so confused that she stammered. "Wh... what?"

"A gun," he repeated. "Do you have any sort of weapon and can you use it?"

"I don't like guns," she said flatly. "Anyway, I won't have one in the house with a six-year-old child, so it's no use telling me to buy one."

He was thinking. His face tautened. "How about self-defense?"

"I teach second grade," she pointed out. "Most of my students don't attack me."

"I'm not worried about you at school. I told you, I don't like the look of your neighbors." He wasn't adding that he knew who they were and why they were in town.

"Neither do I," she admitted. "But it's none of your business..."

"It is," he returned. "I promised Hank that I'd take care of Jess if he ever bought it overseas. I keep my promises."

"I can take care of my aunt."

"Not anymore you can't," he returned, unabashed. "I'm coming over tomorrow."

"I may not be home..."

"Jess will be. Besides, tomorrow is Saturday," he said. "You came in for supplies this afternoon and you don't teach on the weekend. You'll be home." His tone said she'd better be.

She gave an exasperated sound. "Mr. Scott..."

"I'm only Mr. Scott to my enemies," he pointed out.

"Yes, well, Mr. Scott..."

He let out an angry sigh and stared her down. "You were so young," he bit off. "What did you expect me to do, seduce you in the cab of a pickup truck in broad daylight?"

She flushed red as a rose petal. "I wasn't talking about that!"

"It's still in your eyes," he told her quietly. "I'd rather have done it in a way that hadn't left so many scars, but I had to discourage you. The whole damned thing was impossible, you must have realized that by now!"

She hated the embarrassment she felt. "I don't have scars!"

"You do." He studied her oval face, her softly rounded chin, her perfect mouth. "I'll be over tomorrow. I need to talk to you and Jess. There have been some developments that she doesn't know about."

"What sort of developments?"

He closed the hood of the truck and paused by her window. "Drive carefully," he said, ignoring the question. "And get that tire changed."

"I am not a charity case," she said curtly. "I don't take orders. And I definitely do not need some big, strong man to take care of me!"

He smiled, but it wasn't a pleasant smile. He turned on his heel and walked back to his own truck with a stride that was peculiarly his own.

Sally was so shaken that she barely managed to get the truck out of town without stripping the gears out of it.

Jessica Myers was in her bedroom listening to the radio and her son, Stevie, was watching a children's after-school television program when Sally came in. She unloaded the supplies first with the help of her six-year-old cousin.

"You got me that cereal from the TV commercial!" he exclaimed, diving into bags as she put the perishable items into the refrigerator. "Thanks, Aunt Sally!" Although they were cousins, he referred to her as his aunt out of affection and respect.

"You're very welcome. I got some ice cream, too."

"Wow! Can I have some now?"

Sally laughed. "Not until after supper, and you have to eat some of everything I fix. Okay?"

"Aw. Okay, I guess," he muttered, clearly disappointed.

She bent and kissed him between his dark eyes. "That's my good boy. Here, I brought some nice apples and pears. Wash one off and eat it. Fruit is good for you."

"Okay. But it's not as nice as ice cream."

He washed off a pear and carried it into the living room on a paper towel to watch television.

Sally went into Jessica's bedroom, hesitating at the foot of the big four-poster bed. Jessica was slight, blond and hazel-eyed. Her eyes stared at nothing, but she smiled as she recognized Sally's step.

"I heard the truck," she said. "I'm sorry you had to go to town for supplies after working all day and bringing Stevie home first."

"I never mind shopping," Sally said with genuine affection. "You doing all right?"

Jessica shifted on the pillows. She was dressed in sweats, but she looked bad. "I still have some pain from the wreck. I've taken a couple of aspirins for my hip. I thought I'd lie down and give them a chance to work."

Sally came in and sat down in the wing chair beside the

bed. "Jess, Ebenezer Scott asked about you and said he was coming over tomorrow to see you."

Jessica didn't seem at all surprised. She only nodded. "I thought he might," Jessica said quietly. "I had a call from a former colleague about what's going on. I'm afraid I may have landed you in some major trouble, Sally."

"I don't understand."

"Didn't you wonder why I insisted on moving down here so suddenly?"

"Now that you mention it—"

"It was because Ebenezer is here, and we're safer than we would be in Houston."

"Now you're scaring me."

Jessica smiled sadly. "I wouldn't have had this happen for the world. It isn't something that comes up, usually. But these are odd circumstances. A man I helped put in prison is out pending retrial, and he's coming after me."

"You...helped put a man in prison? How?" Sally asked, perplexed.

"You knew that I worked for a government agency?"

"Well, of course. As a clerk."

Jessica took a deep breath. "No, dear. Not as a clerk." She took a deep breath. "I was a special agent for an agency we don't mention publicly. Through Eb and his contacts, I managed to find one of the confidants of drug lord Manuel Lopez, who was head of an international drug cartel. I was given enough hard evidence to send Lopez to prison for drug dealing. I even had copies of his ledgers. But there was one small loophole in the chain of evidence, and the drug lord's attorneys jumped on it. Lopez is now out of prison and he wants the person responsible for helping me put him away. Since I'm the only one who knows the person's identity, I'm the one he'll be coming after."

Sally just sat there, dumbfounded. Things like this only

happened in movies. They certainly didn't happen in real life. Her beloved aunt surely wasn't involved in espionage!

"You're kidding, right?" Sally asked hopefully.

Jessica shook her head slowly. She was still an attractive woman, in her middle thirties. She was slender and she had a sweet face. Stevie, blond and dark-eyed, didn't favor her. Of course, he didn't favor his father, either. Hank had had black hair and light blue eyes.

"I'm sorry, dear," Jessica said heavily. "I'm not kidding. I'm not able to protect myself or you and Stevie anymore, so I had to come home for help. Ebenezer will keep us safe until we can get the drug lord back on ice."

"Is Ebenezer a government agent?" Sally asked, astounded.

"No." Jessica took a deep breath. "I don't like telling you this, and he won't like it, either. It's deeply private. You must swear not to tell another soul."

"I swear." She sat patiently, almost vibrating with curiosity.

"Eb was a professional mercenary," she said. "What they used to call a soldier of fortune. He's led groups of highly trained men in covert operations all over the world. He's retired from that now, but he's still much in demand with our government and foreign governments as a training instructor. His ranch is well-known in covert circles as an academy of tactics and intelligence-gathering."

Sally didn't say a word. She was absolutely speechless. No wonder Ebenezer had been so secretive, so reluctant to let her get close to him. She remembered the tiny white scars on his lean, tanned face, and knew instinctively that there would be more of them under his clothing. No wonder he kept to himself!

"I hope I haven't shattered any illusions, Sally," her aunt said worriedly. "I know how you felt about him."

Sally gaped at her. "You...know?"

Jessica nodded. "Eb told me about that, and about what happened just before you came to live with Hank and me in Houston."

Her face flamed. The shame! She felt sick with humiliation that Ebenezer had known how she felt all the time, and she thought she was doing such a good job of hiding it! She should have realized that it was obvious, when she found excuse after excuse to waylay him in town, when she brazenly climbed into his pickup truck one lovely spring afternoon and pleaded to be taken for a ride. He'd given in to that request, to her surprise. But barely half an hour later, she'd erupted from the passenger seat and run almost all the half-mile down the road to her home. Too ashamed to let anyone see the state she was in, she'd sneaked in the back door and gone straight to her room. She'd never told her parents or anyone else what had happened. Now she wondered if Jessica knew that, too.

"He didn't divulge any secrets, if that's why you're so quiet, Sally," the older woman said gently. "He only said that you had a king-size crush on him and he'd shot you down. He was pretty upset."

That was news. "I wouldn't ever have guessed that he could be upset."

"Neither would I," Jessica said with a smile. "It came as something of a surprise. He told me to keep an eye on you, and check out who you went out with. He could have saved himself the trouble, of course, since you never went out with anyone. He was bitter about that."

Sally averted her face to the window. "He frightened me."

"He knew that. It's why he was bitter."

Sally drew in a steadying breath. "I was very young," she said finally, "and I suppose he did the only thing he could. But I was leaving Jacobsville anyway, when my parents divorced. I only had a week of school before graduation before I went to live with you. He didn't have to go to such lengths.''

"My brother still feels like an idiot for the way he behaved with that college girl he left your mother for," Jessica said curtly, meaning Sally's father, who was Jessica's only living relative besides Sally. "It didn't help that your mother remarried barely six months later. He was stuck with Beverly the Beauty.''

"How are my parents?" Sally asked. It was the first time she'd mentioned either of her parents in a long while, She'd lost touch with them since the divorce that had shattered her life.

"Your father spends most of his time at work while Beverly goes the party route every night and spends every penny he makes. Your mother is separated from her second husband and living in Nassau." Jessica shifted on the bed. "You don't ever hear from your parents, do you?"

"I don't resent them as much as I did. But I never felt that they loved me," she said abruptly. "That's why I felt it was better we went our separate ways.''

"They were children when they married and had you," the other woman said. "Not really mature enough for the responsibility. They resented it, too. That's why you spent so much time with me during the first five years you were alive." Jessica smiled. "I hated it when you went back home.''

"Why did you and Hank wait so long to have a child of your own?" Sally asked.

Jessica flushed. "It wasn't...convenient, with Hank overseas so much. Did you get that tire replaced?" she added, almost as if she were desperate to change the subject.

"You and Mr. Scott!" Sally exploded, diverted. "How did you know it was bald?"

"Because Eb phoned me before you got home and told me to remind you to get it replaced," Jessica chuckled.

"I suppose he has a cell phone in his truck."

"Among other things," Jessica replied with a smile. "He isn't like the men you knew in college or even when you started teaching. Eb is an alpha male," she said quietly. "He isn't politically correct, and he doesn't even pretend to conform. In some ways, he's very old-fashioned."

"I don't feel that way about him anymore," Sally said firmly.

"I'm sorry," Jessica replied gently. "He's been alone most of his life. He needs to be loved."

Sally picked at a cuticle, chipping the clear varnish on her short, neat fingernails. "Does he have family?"

"Not anymore. His mother died when he was very young, and his father was career military. He grew up in the army, you might say. His father was not a gentle sort of man. He died in combat when Eb was in his twenties. There wasn't any other family."

"You said once that you always saw Ebenezer with beautiful women at social events," Sally recalled with a touch of envy.

"He pays for dressing, and he attracts women. But he's careful about his infrequent liaisons. He told me once that he guessed he'd never find a woman who could share the life he leads. He still has enemies who'd like to see him dead," she added.

"Like this drug lord?"

"Yes. Manuel Lopez is a law unto himself. He has millions, and he owns politicians, law enforcement people, even judges," Jessica said irritably. "That's why we were never able to shut him down. Then I was told that a confidant of his wanted to give me information, names and documents that would warrant arresting Lopez on charges of drug trafficking. But I wasn't careful enough. I overlooked one little thing, and Lopez's attorneys used it in a petition for a retrial. They got him out. He's on the loose pending retrial and out for vengeance against his comrade. He'll do anything to get the name of the person who sold him out. Anything at all.''

Sally let her breath out through pursed lips. "So we're all under the gun."

"Exactly. I used to be a crack shot, but without my vision, I'm useless. Eb will have a plan by tomorrow." Her face was solemn as she stared in the general direction of her niece's voice. "Listen to him, Sally. Do exactly what he says. He's our only hope of protecting Stevie."

"I'll do anything I have to, to protect you and Stevie," Sally agreed at once.

"I knew you would."

She toyed with her nails again. "Jess, has Ebenezer ever been serious about anyone?"

"Yes. There was a woman in Houston, in fact, several years ago. He cared for her very much, but she dropped him flat when she found out what he did for a living. She married a much-older bank executive." She shifted on the bed. "I hear that she's widowed now. But I don't imagine he still has any feelings for her. After all, she dropped him, not the reverse."

Sally, who knew something about helpless unrequited love, wasn't so quick to agree. After all, she still had secret feelings for Ebenezer...

"Deep thoughts, dear?" Jessica asked softly.

"I was remembering the reruns we used to see of that old TV series, *The A-Team*," she recalled with an audible laugh. "I loved it when they had to knock out that character Mr. T played to get him on an airplane."

"It was a good show. Not lifelike, of course," Jessica added.

"What part?"

"All of it."

Jessica would probably know, Sally figured. "Why didn't you ever tell me what you did for a living?"

"Need to know," came the dry reply. "You didn't, until now."

"If you knew Ebenezer when he was still working as a mercenary, I guess you learned a lot about the business," she ventured.

Jessica's face closed up. "I learned too much," she said coldly. "Far too much. Men like that are incapable of lasting relationships. They don't know the meaning of love or fidelity."

She seemed to know that, and Sally wondered how. "Was Uncle Hank a mercenary, too?"

"Yes, just briefly," she said. "Hank was never one to rush in and risk killing himself. It was so ironic that he died overseas in his sleep, of a heart condition nobody even knew he had."

That was a surprise, along with all the others that Jessica was getting. Uncle Hank had been very handsome, but not assertive or particularly tough.

"But Ebenezer said he served with Uncle Hank."

"Yes. In basic training, before they joined the Green Berets," Jessica said. "Hank didn't pass the training course. Ebenezer did. In fact," she added amusedly, "he was able to do the Fan Dance."

"Fan Dance?"

"It's a specialized course they put the British commandos, the Special Air Service, guys through. Not many soldiers, even career soldiers, are able to finish it, much less able to pass it on the first try. Eb did. He was briefly 'loaned' to them while he was in army intelligence, for some top secret assignment.''

Sally had never thought very much about Ebenezer's profession, except that she'd guessed he was once in the military. She wasn't sure how she felt about it. A man who'd been in the military might still have a soft spot or two inside. She was almost certain that a commando, a soldier for hire, wouldn't have any.

"You're very quiet," Jessica said.

"I never thought of Ebenezer in such a profession," she replied, moving to look out the window at the November landscape. "I guess it was right there in front of me, and I didn't see it. No wonder he kept to himself."

"He still does," she replied. "And only a few people know about his past. His men do, of course," she added, and there was an inflection in her tone that was suddenly different.

"Do you know any of his men?"

Jessica's face tautened. "One or two. I believe Dallas Kirk still works for him. And Micah Steele does consulting work when Eb asks him to," she added and smiled. "Micah's a good guy. He's the only one of Eb's old colleagues who still works in the trade. He lives in Nassau, but he spends an occasional week helping Ebenezer train men when he's needed."

"And Dallas Kirk?"

Jessica's soft face went very hard. At her side, one of her small hands clenched. "Dallas was badly wounded in a firefight a year ago. He came home shot to pieces and Eb found something for him to teach in the tactics courses. He doesn't speak to me, of course. We had a difficult parting some years ago."

That was intriguing, and Sally was going to find out about it one day. But she didn't press her luck. "How about fajitas for supper?" she asked.

Jessica's glower dissolved into a smile. "Sounds lovely!"

"I'll get right on them." Sally went back into the kitchen, her head spinning with the things she'd learned about people she thought she knew. Life, she considered, was always full of surprises.

Chapter Two

Ebenezer was a man of his word. He showed up early the next morning as Sally was out by the corral fence watching her two beef cattle graze. She'd bought them to raise with the idea of stocking her freezer. Now they had names. The white-faced Black Angus mixed steer was called Bob, the white-faced red-coated Hereford she called Andy. They were pets. She couldn't face the thought of sitting down to a plate of either one of them.

The familiar black pickup stopped at the fence and Ebenezer got out. He was wearing jeans and a blue checked shirt with boots and a light-colored straw Stetson. No chaps, so he wasn't working cattle today.

He joined Sally at the fence. "Don't tell me. They're table beef."

She spared him a resentful glance. "Right."

"And you're going to put them in the freezer."

She swallowed. "Sure."

He only chuckled. He paused to light a cigar, with one

big booted foot propped on the lower rung of the fence. "What are their names?"

"That's Andy and that's...Bob." She flushed.

He didn't say a word, but his raised eyebrow was eloquent through the haze of expelled smoke.

"They're watch-cattle," she improvised.

His eyes twinkled. "I beg your pardon?"

"They're attack steers," she said with a reluctant grin. "At the first sign of trouble, they'll come right through the fence to protect me. Of course, if they get shot in the line of duty," she added, "I'll eat them!"

He pushed his Stetson back over clean blond-streaked brown hair and looked down at her with lingering amusement. "You haven't changed much in six years."

"Neither have you," she retorted shyly. "You're still smoking those awful things."

He glanced at the big cigar and shrugged. "A man has to have a vice or two to round him out," he pointed out. "Besides, I only have the occasional one, and never inside. I have read the studies on smoking," he added dryly.

"Lots of people who smoke read those studies," she agreed. "And then they quit!"

He smiled. "You can't reform me," he told her. "It's a waste of time to try. I'm thirty-six and very set in my ways."

"I noticed."

He took a puff from the cigar and studied her steers. "I suppose they follow you around like dogs."

"When I go inside the fence with them," she agreed. She felt odd with him; safe and nervous and excited, all at once. She could smell the fresh scent of the soap he used, and over it a whiff of expensive cologne. He was close at her side, muscular and vibrating with sensuality. She wanted to move closer, to feel that strength all around her. It made her self-conscious. After six years, surely the attraction should have lessened a little.

He glanced down at her, noticing how she picked at her cuticles and nibbled on her lower lip. His green eyes narrowed and there was a faint glitter in them.

She felt the heat of his gaze and refused to lift her face. She wondered if it looked as hot as it felt.

"You haven't forgotten a thing," he said suddenly, the cigar in his hand absently falling to his side, whirls of smoke climbing into the air beside him.

"About what?" she choked.

He caught her long, blond ponytail and tugged her closer, so that she was standing right up against him. The scent of him, the heat of him, the muscular ripple of his body combined to make her shiver with repressed feelings.

He shifted, coaxing her into the curve of his body, his eyes catching hers and holding them relentlessly. He could feel her faint trembling, hear the excited whip of her breath as she tried valiantly to hide it from him. But he could see her heartbeat jerking the fabric over her small breasts.

It was a relief to find her as helplessly attracted to him as she once had been. It made him arrogant with pride. He let go of the ponytail and drew his hand against her cheek, letting his thumb slide down to her mouth and over her chin to lift her eyes to his.

"To everything, there is a season," he said quietly.

She felt the impact of his steady, unblinking gaze in the most secret places of her body. She didn't have the experience to hide it, to protect herself. She only stood staring up at him, with all her insecurities and fears lying naked in her soft gray eyes.

His head bent and he drew his nose against hers in the sudden silence of the yard. His smoky breath whispered over her lips as he murmured, "Six years is a long time to go hungry."

She didn't understand what he was saying. Her eyes were on his hard, long, thin mouth. Her hands had flattened against his broad chest. Under it she could feel thick, soft hair and the beat of his heart. His breath smelled of cigar smoke and when his mouth gently covered hers, she wondered if she was going to faint with the unexpected delight of it. It had been so long!

He felt her immediate, helpless submission. His free arm went around her shoulders and drew her lazily against his muscular body while his hard mouth moved lightly over her lips, tasting her, assessing her experience. His mouth became insistent and she stiffened a little, unused to the tender probing of his tongue against her teeth.

She felt his smile before he lifted his head.

"You still taste of lemonade and cotton candy," he murmured with unconcealed pleasure.

"What do you mean?" she murmured, mesmerized by the hovering threat of his mouth.

"I mean, you still don't know how to do this." He searched her eyes quietly and then the smile left his face. "I did more damage than I ever meant to. You were seventeen. I had to hurt you to save you." He traced her mouth with his thumb and scowled down at her. "You don't know what my life was like in those days," he said solemnly, and for once his eyes were unguarded. The pain in them was visible for the first time Sally could remember.

"Aunt Jessica told me," she said slowly.

His eyes darkened. His face hardened. "All of it?"

She nodded.

He was still scowling. He released her to gaze off into the distance, absently lifting the cigar to his mouth. He blew out a cloud of smoke. "I'm not sure that I wanted you to know."

"Secrets are dangerous."

He glanced down at her, brooding. "More dangerous than you realize. I've kept mine for a long time, like your aunt."

"I had no idea what she did for a living, either." She glared up at him. "Thanks to the two of you, now I know how a mushroom feels, sitting in the dark."

He chuckled. "She wanted it that way. She felt you'd be safer if she kept you uninvolved."

She wanted to ask him about what Jessica had told her, that he'd phoned her about Sally before the painful move to Houston. But she didn't quite know how. She was shy with him.

He looked down at her again, his eyes intent on her softly flushed cheeks, her swollen mouth, her bright eyes. She lifted his heart. Just the sight of her made him feel welcome, comforted, cared for. He'd missed that. In all his life, Sally had been the first and only person who could thwart his black moods. She made him feel as if he belonged somewhere after a life of wandering. Even during the time she was in Houston, he kept in touch with Jessica, to get news of Sally, of where she was, what she was doing, of her plans. He'd always expected that she'd come back to him one day, or that he'd go to her, despite the way they'd parted. Love, if it existed, was surely a powerful force, immune to harsh words and distance. And time.

Sally's face was watchful, her eyes brimming over with excitement. She couldn't hide what she was feeling, and he loved being able to see it. Her hero worship had first irritated and then elated him. Women had wanted him since his teens, although some loved him for the danger that clung to him. One had rejected him because of it and savaged his pride. But, even so, it was Sally who made him ache inside.

He touched her soft mouth with his fingers, liking the faint swell where he'd kissed it so thoroughly. "We'll have to practice more," he murmured wickedly.

She opened her mouth to protest that assumption when a laughing Stevie came running out the door like a little blond whirlwind, only to be caught up abruptly in Ebenezer's hard arms and lifted.

"Uncle Eb!" he cried, laughing delightedly, making Sally realize that if she hadn't been around Ebenezer since their move from Houston, Jessica and Stevie certainly had.

"Hello, tiger," came the deep, pleasant reply. He put the boy back down on his feet. "Want to go to my place with Sally and learn karate?"

"Like the 'Teenage Mutant Ninja Turtles' in the movies? Radical!" he exclaimed.

"Karate?" Sally asked, hesitating.

"Just a few moves, and only for self-defense," he assured her. "You'll enjoy it. It's necessary," he added when she seemed to hesitate.

"Okay," she capitulated.

He led the way back into the house to where Jessica was sitting in the living room, listening to the news on the television.

"All this mess in the Balkans," she said sadly. "Just when we think we've got peace, everything erupts all over again. Those poor people!"

"Fortunes of war," Eb said with a smile. "How's it going, Jess?"

"I can't complain, I guess, except that they won't let me drive anymore," she said, tongue-in-cheek.

"Wait until they get that virtual reality vision perfected," he said easily. "You'll be able to do anything."

"Optimist," she said, grinning.

"Always. I'm taking these two over to the ranch for a little course in elementary self-defense," he added quietly.

"Good idea," Jessica said at once.

"I don't like leaving you here alone," Sally ventured, remembering what she'd been told about the danger.

"She won't be," Eb replied. He looked at Jessica and one eye narrowed before he added, "I'm sending Dallas Kirk over to keep her company."

"No!" Jessica said furiously. She actually stood up, vibrating. "No, Eb! I don't want him within a mile of me! I'd rather be shot to pieces!"

"This isn't multiple choice," came a deep, drawling voice from the general direction of the hall.

As Sally turned from Jessica's white face, a slender blond man with dark eyes came into the room. He walked with the help of a fancy-looking cane. He was dressed like Eb, in casual clothes, khaki slacks and a bush jacket. He looked like something right out of Africa.

"This is Dallas Kirk," Eb introduced him to Sally. "He was born in Texas. His real name is Jon, but we've always called him Dallas. This is Sally Johnson," he told the blond man.

Dallas nodded. "Nice to meet you," he said formally.

"You know Jess," Eb added.

"Yes. I...know her," he said with the faintest emphasis in that lazy Western drawl, during which Jess's face went from white to scarlet and she averted her eyes.

"Surely you can get along for an hour," Eb said impatiently. "I really can't leave you here by yourself, Jess."

Dallas glared at her. "Mind telling me why?" he asked Eb. "She's a better shot than I am."

Jessica stood rigidly by her chair. "He doesn't know?" she asked Eb.

Eb's face was rigid. "He wouldn't talk about you, and the subject didn't come up until he was away on assignment. No. He doesn't know."

"Know what?" Dallas demanded.

Jessica's chin lifted. "I'm blind," she said matter-of-factly, almost with satisfaction, as if she knew it would hurt him.

The look on the newcomer's face was a revelation. Sally only wished she knew of what. He shifted as if he'd sustained a physical blow. He walked slowly up to her and waved a hand in front of her face.

"Blind!" he said huskily. "For how long?"

"Six months," she said, feeling for the arms of the chair. She sat back down a little clumsily. "I was in a wreck. An accident," she added abruptly.

"It was no accident," Eb countered coldly. "She was run off the road by two of Lopez's men. They got away before the police came."

Sally gasped. This was a new explanation. She'd just heard about the wreck—not about the cause of it. Dallas's hand on the cane went white from the pressure he was exerting on it. "What about Stevie?" he asked coldly. "Is he all right? Was he injured?"

"He wasn't with me at the time. And he's fine. Sally lives with us and helps take care of him," Jess replied, her voice unusually tense. "We share the chores. She's my niece," she added abruptly, almost as if to warn him of something.

Dallas looked preoccupied. But when Stevie came running back into the room, he turned abruptly and his eyes widened as he stared at the little boy.

"I'm ready!" Stevie announced, holding out his arms

to show the gray sweats he was wearing. His dark eyes were shimmering with joy. "This is how they look on television when they practice. Is it okay?"

"It's fine," Eb replied with a smile.

"Who's he?" Stevie asked, big-eyed, as he looked at the blond man with the cane who was staring at him, as if mesmerized.

"That's Dallas," Eb said easily. "He works for me."

"Hi," Stevie said, naturally outgoing. He stared at the cane. "I guess you're from Texas with a name like that, huh? I'm sorry about your leg, Mr. Dallas. Does it hurt much?"

Dallas took a slow breath before he answered. "When it rains."

"My mama's hip hurts when it rains, too," he said. "Are you coming with us to learn karate?"

"He's already forgotten more than I know," Eb said in a dry tone. "No, he's going to take care of your mother while we're gone."

"Why?" Stevie asked, frowning.

"Because her hip hurts," Sally lied through her teeth. "Ready to go?"

"Sure! Bye, Mom." He ran to kiss her cheek and be hugged warmly. He moved back, smiling up at the blond man who hadn't cracked a smile yet. "See you."

Dallas nodded.

Sally was staggered by the resemblance of the boy to the man, and almost remarked on it. But before she could, Eb caught her eyes. There was a look in them that she couldn't decipher, but it stopped her at once.

"We'd better go," he said. He took Sally by the arm. "Come on, Stevie. We won't be long, Jess," he called back.

"I'll count the seconds," she said under her breath as they left the room.

Dallas didn't say anything, and it was just as well that she couldn't see the look in his eyes.

It was impossible to talk in front of Stevie as they drove through the massive electronic gates at the Scott ranch. He, like Sally, was fascinated by the layout, which included a helipad, a landing strip with a hangar, a swimming pool and a ranch house that looked capable of sleeping thirty people. There were also target ranges and guest cabins and a formidable state-of-the-art gym housed in what looked like a gigantic Quonset hut like those used during the Second World War in the Pacific theater. There were several satellite dishes as well, and security cameras seemingly on every available edifice.

"This is incredible," Sally said as they got out of the truck and went with him toward the gym.

"Maintaining it is incredible," Eb said with a chuckle. "You wouldn't believe the level of technology required to keep it all functioning."

Stevie had found the thick blue plastic-covered mat on the wood floor and was already rolling around on it and trying the punching bag suspended from one of the steel beams that supported other training equipment.

"Stevie looks like that man, Dallas," she said abruptly.

He grimaced. "Haven't you and Jess ever talked?"

"I didn't know anything about Dallas and my aunt until you told me," she said simply.

"This is something she needs to tell you, in her own good time."

She studied the youngster having fun on the mat. "He isn't my uncle's child, is he?"

There was a rough sound from the man beside her. "What makes you think so?"

"For one thing, because he's the image of Dallas. But also because Uncle Hank and Aunt Jessie were married for years with no kids, and suddenly she got pregnant just before he died overseas," she replied. "Stevie was like a miracle."

"In some ways, I suppose he was. But it led to Hank asking for a combat assignment, and even though he died of a heart condition, Jess has had nightmares ever since out of guilt." He looked down at her. "You can't tell her that you know."

"Fair enough. Tell me the rest."

"She and Dallas were working together on an assignment. It was one of those lightning attractions that overcome the best moral obstacles. They were alone too much and finally the inevitable happened. Jess turned up pregnant. When Dallas found out, he went crazy. He demanded that Jess divorce Hank and marry him, but she wouldn't. She swore that Dallas wasn't the father of her child, Hank was, and she had no intention of divorcing her husband."

"Oh, dear."

"Hank knew that she'd been with another man, of course, because he'd always been sterile. Dallas didn't know that. And Hank hadn't told Jessica until she announced that she was expecting a child." He shrugged. "He wouldn't forgive her. Neither would Dallas. When Hank died, Dallas didn't even try to get in touch with Jess. He really believed that Stevie was Hank's child. Until about ten minutes ago, that is," he added with a wry smile. "It didn't take much guesswork for him to see the resemblance. I think we won't go back for a couple of hours. I don't want to walk into the firefight he's probably having with Jess even as we speak."

She bit her lower lip. "Poor Jess."

"Poor Dallas," he countered. "After the fight with Jessie, he took every damned dangerous assignment he could find, the more dangerous the better. Last year in Africa, Dallas was shot to pieces. They sent him home with wounds that would have killed a lesser man."

"No wonder he looks so bitter."

"He's bitter because he loved Jess and though she felt the same, she wasn't willing to hurt Hank by leaving him. But in the end, she still hurt him. He couldn't live with the idea that she was having some other man's child. It destroyed their marriage."

She grimaced. "What a tragedy, for all of them."

"Yes."

She looked toward Stevie, smiling. "He's a great kid," she said. "I'd love him even if he wasn't my first cousin."

"He's got grit and personality to boot."

"You wouldn't think so at midnight when you're still trying to get him to sleep."

He smiled as he studied her. "You love kids, don't you?"

"Oh, yes," she said fervently. "I love teaching."

"Don't you want some of your own?" he asked with a quizzical smile.

She flushed and wouldn't look at him. "Sure. One day."

"Why not now?"

"Because I've already got more responsibilities than I can manage. Pregnancy would be a complication I couldn't handle, especially now."

"You sound as if you're planning to do it all alone."

She shrugged. "There is such a thing as artificial insemination."

He turned her toward him, looking very solemn and

adult. "How would it feel, carrying the child of a man you didn't even know, having it grow inside your body?"

She bit her lower lip. She hadn't considered the intimacy of what he was suggesting. She felt, and looked, confused.

"A baby should be made out of love, the natural way, not in a test tube," he said very softly, searching her shocked eyes. "Well, not unless it's the only way two people can have a child," he added. "But that's an entirely different circumstance."

Her lips parted on the surge of emotion that made her heart race. "I don't know…that I want to get that close to anyone, ever."

He seemed even more remote. "Sally, you can't let the past lock you into solitude forever. I frightened you because I wanted to keep you at bay. If I didn't discourage you somehow I was afraid that the temptation might prove too much for me. You were such a baby." He scowled bitterly. "What happened wouldn't have been so devastating if you'd had even a little experience with men. For God's sake, didn't they ever let you date anyone?"

She shook her head, her teeth clenched tightly together. "My mother was certain that I'd get pregnant or catch some horrible disease. She talked about it all the time. She made boys who came to the house so uncomfortable that they never came back."

"I didn't know that," he said tautly.

"Would it have made any difference?" she asked miserably.

He touched her face with cool, firm fingers. "Yes. I wouldn't have gone nearly as far as I did, if I'd known."

"You wanted to get rid of me…"

He put his thumb over her soft mouth. "I wanted you," he whispered huskily. "But a seventeen-year-old isn't mature enough for a love affair. And that would have been impossible in Jacobsville, even if I'd been crazy enough to go all the way with you that day. You were almost thirteen years my junior.''

She was beginning to see things from his point of view. She hadn't tried before. There had been so much resentment, so much bitterness, so much hurt. She looked at him and saw, for the first time, the pain of the memory in his face.

"I was desperate," she said, speaking softly. "They told me out of the blue that they were divorcing each other. They were selling the house and moving out of town. Dad was going to marry Beverly, this girl he'd met at the college where he taught. Mom couldn't live in the same town with everybody knowing that Dad had thrown her over for someone younger. She married a man she hardly knew shortly afterward, just to save her pride.'' She stared at his mouth with more hunger than she realized. "I knew that I'd never see you again. I only wanted you to kiss me.'' She swallowed, averting her eyes. "I must have been crazy.''

"We both were." He cupped her face in his hands and lifted it to his quiet eyes. "For what it's worth, I never meant it to go further than a kiss. A very chaste kiss, at that.'' His eyes drifted down involuntarily to the soft thrust of her breasts almost touching his shirt. He raised an eyebrow at the obvious points. "That's why it wasn't chaste.''

She didn't understand. "What is?''

He looked absolutely exasperated. "How can you be that old and know nothing?'' he asked. He glanced over her shoulder at Stevie, who was facing the other way and giving the punching bag hell. He took Sally's own finger and drew it across her taut breast. He looked straight into her eyes as he said softly, "That's why.''

She realized that it must have something to do with

being aroused, but no one had ever told her blatantly that it was a visible sign of desire. She went scarlet.

"You greenhorn," he murmured indulgently. "What a babe in arms."

"I don't read those sort of books," she said haughtily.

"You should. In fact, I'll buy you a set of them. Maybe a few videos, too," he murmured absently, watching the expressions come and go on her face.

"You varmint...!"

He caught her top lip in both of his and ran his tongue lazily under it. She stiffened, but her hands were clinging to him, not pushing.

"You remember that, don't you, Sally?" he murmured with a smile. "Do you remember what comes next?"

She jerked back from him, staggering. Her eyes found Stevie, still oblivious to the adults.

Eb's eyes were blatant on the thrust of her breasts and he was smiling.

She crossed her arms over her chest and glared up at him. "You just stop that," she gritted. "I'll bet you weren't born knowing everything!"

He chuckled. "No, I wasn't. But I didn't have a mother to keep my nose clean, either," he said. "My old man was military down to his toenails, and he didn't believe in gentle handling or delicacy. He used women until the day he died." He laughed coldly. "He told me that there was no such thing as a good woman, that they were to be enjoyed and put aside."

She was appalled. "Didn't he love your mother?"

"He wanted her, and she wouldn't be with him until they got married," he said simply. "So they got married. She died having me. They were living in a small town outside the military base where he was stationed. He was overseas on assignment and she lived alone, isolated. She went into labor and there were complications. There was nothing that could have been done for her by the time she was found. If a neighbor hadn't come to look in on us, I'd have died with her."

"It must have been a shock for your father," she said.

"If it was, it never showed. He left me with a cousin until I was old enough to obey orders, then I went to live with him. I learned a lot from him, but he wasn't a loving man." His eyes narrowed on her soft face. "I followed his example and joined the army. I was lucky enough to get into the Green Berets. Then when I was due for discharge, a man approached me about a top secret assignment and told me what it would pay." He shrugged. "Money is a great temptation for a young man with a domineering father. I said yes and he never spoke to me again. He said that what I was doing was a perversion of the military, and that I wasn't fit to be any officer's son. He disowned me on the spot. I didn't hear from him again. A few years later, I got a letter from his post commander, stating that he'd died in combat. He had a military funeral with full honors."

The pain of those years was in his lean, hard face. Impulsively she put a hand on his arm. "I'm sorry," she told him quietly. "He must have been the sort of man who only sees one side of any argument."

He was surprised by her compassion. "Don't you think mercenaries are evil, Miss Purity?" he asked sarcastically.

Chapter Three

Sally looked up into pain-laced green eyes and without thinking, she lifted her hand from his arm and raised it toward his hard cheek. But when she realized what she was doing, she drew it back at once.

"No, I don't think mercenaries are evil," she said quickly, embarrassed by the impulsive gesture that, thankfully, he didn't seem to notice. "There are a lot of countries where atrocities are committed, whose governments don't have the manpower or resources to protect their people. So, someone else gets hired to do it. I don't think it's a bad thing, when there's a legitimate cause."

He was surprised by her matter-of-fact manner. He'd wondered for years how she might react when she learned about what he did for a living. He'd expected everything from revulsion to shock, especially when he remembered how his former fiancée had reacted to the news. But Sally wasn't squeamish or judgmental.

He'd seen her hand jerk back and it had wounded him.

But now, on hearing her opinion of his work, his heart lifted. "I didn't expect you to credit me with noble motives."

"They are, though, aren't they?" she asked confidently.

"As a matter of fact, in my case, they are," he replied. "Even in my green days, I never did it just for the money. I had to believe in what I was risking my life for."

She grinned. "I thought maybe it was like on television," she confessed. "But Jess said it was nothing like fiction."

He cocked an eyebrow. "Oh, I wouldn't say that," he mused. "Parts of it are."

"Such as?"

"We had a guy like 'B.A. Barrabas' in one unit I led," he said. "We really did have to knock him out to get him on a plane. But he quit the group before we got inventive."

She laughed. "Too bad. You'd have had plenty of stories to tell about him."

He was quiet for a moment, studying her.

"Do I have a zit on my nose?" she asked pleasantly.

He reached out and caught the hand she'd started to lift toward him earlier and kissed its soft palm. "Let's get to work," he said, pulling her along to the mat. "I'll change into my sweats and we'll cover the basics. We won't have a lot of time," he added dryly. "I expect Jess to call very soon with an ultimatum about Dallas."

Jess and Dallas had squared off, in fact, the minute they heard the truck crank and pull out of the yard.

Dallas glared at her from his superior height, leaning heavily on his cane. He wished she could see him, because his eyes were full of anger and bitterness.

"Did you think I wouldn't see that Stevie is the living image of me? My son," he growled at her. "You had my

son! And you lied to me about it and wouldn't ask Hank
for a divorce!''

"I couldn't!'' she exclaimed. "For heaven's sake, he
adored me. He'd never have cheated on me. I couldn't
bring myself to tell him that I'd had an affair with his best
friend!''

"I could have told him,'' he returned furiously. "He
was no angel, Jess, despite the wings you're trying to paint
on him. Or do you think he never strayed on those overseas
jaunts?'' he chided.

She stiffened. "That's not true!''

"It is true!'' he replied angrily. "He knew he couldn't
get anybody pregnant, and he was sure you'd never find
out.''

She put a hand to her head. She'd never dreamed that
Hank had cheated on her. She'd felt so guilty, when all
the time, he was doing the same thing—and then judging
her brutally for what she'd done. "I didn't know,'' she
said miserably.

"Would it have made a difference?''

"I don't know. Maybe it would have.'' She smoothed
the dress over her legs. "You thought Stevie was yours
from the beginning, didn't you?''

"No. I didn't know Hank was sterile until later on. You
told me the child was Hank's and I believed you. Hell, by
then, I couldn't even be sure that it was his.''

"You didn't think—'' She stopped abruptly. "Oh, dear
God, you thought you were one in a line?'' she exploded,
horrified. "You thought I ran around on Hank with any
man who asked me?''

"I knew very little about you except that you knocked
me sideways,'' he said flatly. "I knew Hank ran around
on you. I assumed you were allowed the same freedom.''
He turned away and walked to the window, staring out at

the flat horizon. "I asked you to divorce Hank just to see what you'd say. It was exactly what I expected. You had it made—a husband who tolerated your unfaithfulness, and no danger of falling in love."

"I thought I had a good marriage until you came along," she said bitterly.

He turned, his eyes blazing. "Don't make it sound cheap, Jess," he said harshly. "Neither of us could stop that night. Neither of us tried."

She put her face in her hands and shivered. The memory of how it had been could still reduce her to tears. She'd been in love for the first time in her life, but not with her husband. This man had haunted her ever since. Stevie was the mirror image of him.

"I was so ashamed," she choked. "I betrayed Hank. I betrayed everything I believed in about loyalty and duty and honor. I felt like a Saturday night special at the bordello afterward."

He scowled. "I never treated you that way," he said harshly.

"Of course you didn't!" she said miserably, wiping at tears. "But I was raised to believe that people got married and never cheated on each other. I was a virgin when I married Hank, and nobody in my whole family was ever divorced until Sally's father, my brother, was." She shook her head, oblivious to the expression that washed over Dallas's hard, lean face. "My parents were happily married for fifty years before they died."

"Sometimes it doesn't work," he said flatly, but in a less hostile tone. "That's nobody's fault."

She smoothed back her short hair and quickly wiped away the tears. "Maybe not."

He moved back toward her and sat down in a chair across from hers, putting the cane down on the floor. He leaned forward with a hard sigh and looked at Jessica's pale, wan face with bitterness while he tried to find the words.

She heard the cane as he placed it on the floor. "Eb said you were badly hurt overseas," she said softly, wishing with all her heart that she could see him. "Are you all right?"

That husky softness in her tone, that exquisite concern, was almost too much for him. He grasped her slender hands in his and held them tightly. "I'm better off than you seem to be," he said heavily. "What a hell of a price we paid for that night, Jess."

She felt the hot sting of tears. "It was very high," she had to admit. She reached out hesitantly to find his face. Her fingers traced it gently, finding the new scars, the new hardness of its elegant lines. "Stevie looks like you," she said softly, her unseeing eyes so full of emotion that he couldn't bear to look into them.

"Yes."

She searched her darkness with anguish for a face she would never see again. "Don't be bitter," she pleaded. "Please don't hate me."

He pulled her hand away as if it scalded him. "I've done little else for the past five years," he said flatly. "But maybe you're right. All the rage in the world won't change the past." He let go of her hand. "We have to pick up the pieces and go on."

She hesitated. "Can we at least be friends?"

He laughed coldly. "Is that what you want?"

She nodded. "Eb says you've given up overseas assignments and that you're working for him. I want you to get to know Stevie," she added quietly. "Just in case..."

"Oh, for God's sake, stop it!" he exploded, rising awkwardly from the chair with the help of the cane. "Lopez won't get you. We aren't going to let anything happen to you."

She leaned back in her chair without replying. They both knew that Lopez had contacts everywhere and that he never gave up. If he wanted her dead, he could get her. She didn't want her child left alone in the world.

"I'm going to make some coffee," Dallas said tautly, refusing to think about the possibility of a world without her in it. "What do you take in yours?"

"I don't care," she said indifferently.

He didn't say another word. He went into the kitchen and made a pot of coffee while Jessica sat stiffly in her own living room and contemplated the direction her life had taken.

"You have got…to be kidding!" Sally choked as she dragged herself up from the mat for the twentieth time. "You mean I'm going to spend two hours falling down? I thought you were going to teach me self-defense!"

"I am," Eb replied easily. He, too, was wearing sweats now, and he'd been teaching her side breakfalls, first left and then right. "First you learn how to fall properly, so you don't hurt yourself landing. Then we move on to stances, hand positions and kicks. One step at a time."

She swept her arm past her hip and threw herself down on her side, falling with a loud thud but landing neatly. Beside her, Stevie was going at it with a vengeance and laughing gleefully.

"Am I doing it right?" she puffed, already perspiring. She was very much out of condition, despite the work she did around the house.

He nodded. "Very nice. Be careful about falling too close to the edge of the mat, though. The floor's hard."

She moved further onto the mat and did it again.

"If you think these are fun," he mused, "wait until we do forward breakfalls."

She gaped at him. "You mean I'm going to have to fall deliberately on my face? I'll break my nose!"

"No, you won't," he said, moving her aside. "Watch."

He executed the movement to perfection, catching his weight neatly on his hands and forearms. He jumped up again. "See? Simple."

"For you," she agreed, her eyes on the muscular body that was as fit as that of a man half his age. "Do you train all the time?"

"I have to," he said. "If I let myself get out of shape, I won't be of any use to my students. Great job, Stevie," he called to the boy, who beamed at him.

"Of course he's doing a great job," she muttered. "He's so close to the ground already that he doesn't have far to fall!"

"Poor old lady," he chided gently.

She glared in his direction as she swept her arm forward and threw herself down again. "I'm not old. I'm just out of condition."

He looked at her, sprawled there on the mat, and his lips pursed as he sketched every inch of her. "Funny, I'd have said you were in prime condition. And not just for karate."

She cleared her throat and got to her feet again. "When did you start learning this stuff?"

"When I was in grammar school," he said. "My father taught me."

"No wonder it looks so easy when you do it."

"I train hard. It's saved my life a few times."

She studied his scarred face with curiosity. She could see the years in it, and the hardships. She knew very little about military operations, except for what she'd seen in movies and on television. And as Jess had told her, it wasn't like that in real life. She tried to imagine an armed adversary coming at her and she stiffened.

"Something wrong?" he asked gently.

"I was trying to imagine being attacked," she said. "It makes me nervous."

"It won't, when you gain a little confidence. Stand up straight," he said. "Never walk with your head down in a slumped posture. Always look as if you know where you're going, even if you don't. And always, always, run if you can. Never stand and fight unless you're trapped and your life is in danger."

"Run? You're kidding, of course?"

"No," he said. "I'll give you an example. A man of any size and weight on drugs is more than a match for any three other men. What I'm going to teach you might work on an untrained adversary who's sober. But a man who's been drinking, or especially a man who's using drugs can kill you outright, regardless of what I can teach you. Don't you ever forget that. Overconfidence kills."

"I'll bet you don't teach your men to run," she said accusingly.

His eyes were quiet and full of bad memories. "Sally, a recruit in one of my groups emptied the magazine of his rifle into an enemy soldier on drugs at point-blank range. The enemy kept right on coming. He killed the recruit before he finally fell dead himself."

Her lower jaw fell.

"That was my reaction, too," he informed her. "Absolute disbelief. But it's true. If anyone high on drugs comes at you, don't try to reason with him…you can't. And don't try to fight him. Run like hell. If a full automatic clip won't bring a man down, you certainly can't. Neither can even a combat-hardened man, alone. In that sort of situation, it's just basic common sense to get out of the way as quickly as possible if there's any chance of escape, and pride be damned.''

"I'll remember," she said, all her confidence vanishing. She could see in Eb's eyes that he'd watched that recruit die, and had to live with the memory forever in his mind. Probably it was one of many nightmarish episodes he'd like to forget.

"Sometimes retreat really is the better part of valor," he said, smiling.

"You're educational."

He smiled slowly. "Am I, now?" he asked, and the way he looked at her didn't have much to do with teaching her self-defense. "I can think of a few areas where you need...improvement."

She glanced at Stevie, who was still falling on the mat. "You shouldn't try to shoot ducks in a barrel," she told him. "It's unsporting."

"Shooting is not what I have in mind."

She cleared her throat. "I suppose I should try falling some more." She brightened. "Say, if I learn to do this well, I could try falling on an adversary!"

"Ineffective unless you want to gain three hundred pounds," he returned. He grinned. "Although, you could certainly experiment on me, if you want to. It might immobilize me. We won't know until we try it. Want me to lie down and let you practice?" he added with twinkling eyes.

She laughed, but nervously. "I don't think I'm ready to try that right away."

"Suit yourself. No hurry. We've got plenty of time."

She remembered Jess and the drug lord and her eyes grew worried. "Is it really dangerous for us at home...?"

He held up a cautioning hand. "Stevie, how about a soft drink?"

"That would be great!"

"There are some cans of soda in the fridge in the kitchen. How about bringing one for me and your aunt as well?"

"Sure thing!"

Stevie took off like a bullet.

"Yes, it's dangerous," Eb said quietly. "You aren't to go alone, anywhere, at night. I'll always have a man watching the house, but if you have to go to a meeting or some such thing, let me know and I'll go with you."

"Won't that cramp your social life?" she asked without quite meeting his eyes.

"I don't have a social life," he said with a faint smile. "Not of the sort you're talking about."

"Oh."

His face tautened. "Neither do you, if I can believe Jess."

She shifted on the mat. "I haven't really had much time for men."

"You don't have to spare my feelings," he told her quietly. "I know I've caused you some sleepless nights. But you've waited too long to deal with it. The longer you wait, the harder it's going to be to form a relationship with a man."

"I have Jess and Stevie to think about."

"That's an excuse. And not a very good one."

She felt uncomfortable with her memories. She wrapped her arms around her chest and looked at him with shattered dreams in her eyes.

He took a sharp breath. "It will never be like that again," he said curtly. "I promise you it won't."

She averted her eyes to the mat. "Do you think Jess

and Dallas have done each other in by now?'' she asked, trying to change the subject.

He moved closer, watching her stiffen, watching her draw away from him mentally. His big, lean hands caught her shoulders and he made her look at him.

''You're older now,'' he said, his voice steady and low. ''You should know more about men than you did, even if you've had to learn it through books and television. I was fiercely aroused that day, it had been a long, dry spell, and you were seventeen years old. Get the picture?''

For the first time, she did. Her eyes searched his, warily, and nodded.

His hands contracted on her soft arms. ''You might try it again,'' he said softly.

''Try what?''

''What you did that afternoon,'' he murmured, smiling tenderly. ''Wearing sexy clothes and perfume and making a beeline for me. Anything could happen.''

Her eyes were sadder than she realized as she met his even gaze. ''I'm not the same person I was then,'' she told him. ''But you still are.''

The light seemed to go out of him. His pale eyes narrowed, fastened to hers. ''No,'' he said after a minute. ''I've changed, too. I lost my taste for commando work a long time ago. I teach tactics now. That's all I do.''

''You're not a family man,'' she replied bravely.

Something changed in his face, in his eyes, as he studied her. ''I've thought about that a lot recently,'' he contradicted. ''About a home and children. I might have to give up some of the contract work I do, once the kids came along. I won't allow my children anywhere near weapons. But I can always write field manuals and train teachers in tactics and strategy and intelligence-gathering,'' he added.

"You don't know that you could settle for that," she pointed out.

"Not until I try," he agreed. His gaze fell to her soft mouth and lingered there. "But then, no man really wants to tie himself down. It takes a determined woman to make him want it."

She felt as if he were trying to tell her something, but before she could ask him to clarify what he'd said, Stevie was back with an armful of soft drinks and the moment was lost.

Jess and Dallas weren't speaking at all when the others arrived. Dallas was toying with a cup of cold coffee, looking unapproachable. When Eb came in the door, Dallas went out it, without a word or a backward glance.

"I don't need to ask how it went," Eb murmured.

"It would be pretty pointless," Jessica said dully.

"Mama, I learned to do breakfalls! I wish I could show you," Stevie said, climbing into his mother's lap and hugging her.

She fought tears as she cuddled him close and kissed his sweaty forehead. "Good for you! You listen when Eb tells you something. He's very good."

"Stevie's a natural," Eb chuckled. "In fact, so is your niece." He gave Sally a slow going-over with his eyes.

"She's a quick learner," Jessica said. "Like I was, once."

"I have to get back," Eb said. "There's nothing to worry about right now," he added, careful not to speak too bluntly in front of the child. "I have everything in hand. But I have told Sally to let me know if she plans to go out alone at night, for any reason."

"I will," Sally promised. She didn't want to risk her aunt's life, or Stevie's, by being too independent.

Eb nodded. "We'll keep the lessons up át least three times a week," he told Sally. "I want to move you into self-defense pretty quickly."

She understood why and felt uneasy. "Okay."

"Don't worry," he said gently. "Everything's going to be fine. I know exactly what I'm doing."

She managed a smile for him. "I know that."

"Walk me to the door," he coaxed. "See you, Jess."

"Take care, Eb," Jessie replied, her goodbye echoed by her son's.

On the front porch, Eb closed the door and looked down into Sally's wide gray eyes with concern and something more elusive.

"I'll have the house watched," he promised. "But you have to be careful about even normal things like opening the door when someone comes. Always keep the chain lock on until you know who's out there. Another thing, you have to keep your doors and windows locked, curtains drawn and an escape route always in mind."

She bit her lip worriedly. "I've never had to deal with anything like this."

His big, warm hands closed over her shoulders. "I know. I'm sorry that you and Stevie have been put in the line of fire along with Jess. But you can handle this," he said confidently. "You're strong. You can do whatever you have to do."

She searched his hard, lean face, saw the deep lines and scars that the violence of his life had carved into it, and knew that he would never lie to her. Her frown dissolved. His confidence in her made her feel capable of anything. She smiled.

He smiled back and traced a lazy line from her cheek down to her soft mouth. "If Stevie wasn't so unpredictable, I'd kiss you," he said quietly. "I like your mouth under mine."

Her caught breath was audible. There had never been anyone who could do to her with words what he could.

He traced her lips, entranced. "I used to dream about that afternoon with you," he said in a sensuous tone. "I woke up sweating, swearing, hating myself for what I'd done." He laughed hollowly. "Hating you for what I'd done, too," he added. "I blamed us both. But I couldn't forget how it was."

She colored delicately and lowered her eyes to his broad chest under the shirt he wore. The memories were so close to the surface of her mind that it was impossible not to glimpse them from time to time. Now, they were blatant and embarrassing.

His lean hands moved up to frame her face and force her eyes to meet his. He wasn't smiling.

"No other man will ever have the taste of you that I did, that day," he said roughly. "You were so deliciously innocent."

Her lips parted at the intensity of his tone, at the faint glitter of his green eyes. "That isn't what you said at the time!" she accused.

"At the time," he murmured huskily, watching her mouth, "I was hurting so much that I didn't take time to choose my words. I just wanted you out of the damned truck before I started stripping you out of those tight little shorts you were wearing."

The flush in her cheeks got worse. The image of it was unbelievably shocking. Somehow, it had never occurred to her that at some point he might undress her, to gain access...

"What an expression," he said, chuckling in spite of

himself. "Hadn't you considered what might happen when you came on to me that hard?"

She shook her head.

His fingers slid into the blond hair at her temples where the long braid pulled it away from her face. "Someone should have had a long talk with you."

"You did," she recalled nervously.

"Long and explicit, the day afterward," he said, nodding. "You didn't want to hear it, but I made you. I liked to think that it might have saved you from an even worse experience."

"It wasn't exactly a bad experience," she said, staring at his shirt button. "That was part of the problem."

There was a long, static silence. "Sally," he breathed, and his mouth moved down slowly to cover hers in the silence of the porch.

She stood on tiptoe to coax him closer, lost in the memory of that long-ago afternoon. She felt his hands on her arms, guiding them up around his neck before they fell back to her hips and lifted her into the suddenly swollen contours of his muscular body.

She gasped, giving him the opening he wanted, so that he could deepen the kiss. She felt the warm hardness of his mouth against hers, the soft nip of his teeth, the deep exploration of his tongue. A warm flood of sensation rushed into her lower abdomen and she felt her whole body go tense with it. It was as if her body had become perfectly attuned to this man's years ago, and could never belong to anyone else.

He felt her headlong response and slowly let her back down, lifting his mouth away from hers. He studied her face, her swollen, soft mouth, her wide eyes, her dazed expression.

"Yes," he said huskily.

"Yes?"

He bent and nipped her lower lip sensuously before he pushed her away.

She stared up at him helplessly, feeling as if she'd just been dropped from a great height.

His eyes went to her breasts and lingered on the sharp little points so noticeable at the front of her blouse, the fabric jumping with every hard, quick beat of her heart.

She met that searching gaze and felt the power of it all the way to her toes.

"You know as well as I do that it's only a matter of time," he said softly. "It always has been."

She frowned. Her mind seemed to have shut down. She couldn't quite focus, and her legs felt decidedly weak.

His eyes were back on her breasts, swerving to the closed door, and to both curtained windows before he stepped in close and cupped her blatantly in his warm, sensuous hands.

Sally's mouth opened on a shocked gasp that became suddenly a moan of pleasure.

"I won't hurt you," he whispered, and his mouth covered hers hungrily.

It was the most passionate, adult kiss of her life, even eclipsing what had come before. His hands found their way under her sweatshirt and against lace-covered soft flesh. Her body responded instantly to the slow caresses. She curled into his body, eagerly submissive.

"Lord, what I wouldn't give to unfasten this," he groaned at her mouth as his fingers toyed with the closure at her back. "And sure as hell, Stevie would come outside the minute I did, and show and tell would take on a whole new meaning."

The idea of it amused him and he lifted his head, smiling down into Sally's equally laughing eyes.

"Ah, well," he said, removing his hands with evident reluctance. "All things come to those who wait," he added.

Sally blushed and moved a little away from him.

"Don't be embarrassed," he chided gently, his green eyes sparkling, full of mischief and pleasure. "All of us have a weak spot."

"Not you, man of steel," she teased.

"We'll talk about that next time," he said. "Meanwhile, remember what I said. Especially about night trips."

"Now where would I go alone at night in Jacobsville?" she asked patiently.

He only laughed. But even as she watched him drive away she remembered an upcoming parents and teachers meeting. There would be plenty of time to tell him about that, she reminded herself. She turned back into the house, her mouth and body still tingling pleasantly.

Chapter Four

Jessica was subdued after the time she'd spent with Dallas. Even Stevie noticed, and became more attentive. Sally cooked her aunt's favorite dishes and did her best to coax Jess into a better frame of mind. But the other woman's sadness was blatant.

With her mind on Jessica and not on time passing, she forgot that she had a parents and teachers meeting the next Tuesday night. She phoned Eb's ranch, as she'd been told to, but all she got was the answering machine and a message that only asked the caller to leave a name and number. She left a message, doubting that he'd hear it before she was safely home. She hadn't really believed him when he'd said the whole family was in danger, especially since nothing out of the ordinary had happened. But even so, surely nothing was going to happen to her on a two-mile drive home!

She sent Stevie home with a fellow teacher. The business meeting was long and explosive, and it was much later than usual when it was finally over. Sally spoke to the parents she knew and left early. She wasn't thinking about anything except her bed as she drove down the long, lonely road toward home. As she passed the large house and accompanying acreage where her three neighbors lived, she felt a chill. Three of them were out on their front porch. The light was on, and it looked as if they were arguing about something. They caught sight of her truck and there was an ominous stillness about them.

Sally drove faster, aware that she drew their attention as she went past them. Only a few more minutes, she thought, and she'd be home...

The steering wheel suddenly became difficult to turn and with horror she heard the sound of a tire going flatter and flatter. Her heart flipped over. She didn't have a spare. She'd rolled it out of the bed to make room for the cattle feed she'd taken home last week, having meant to ask Eb to help her put it back in again. But she'd have to walk the rest of the way, now. Worse, it was dark and those creepy men were still watching the truck.

Well, she told herself as she climbed out of the cab with her purse over her shoulder, they weren't going to give her any trouble. She had a loud whistling device, and she now knew enough at least self-defense to protect herself. Confident, despite Eb's earlier warnings, she locked the truck and started walking.

The sound of running feet came toward her. She looked over her shoulder and stopped, turning, her mouth set in a grim line. Two of the three men were coming down the road toward her in a straight line. Just be calm, she told herself. She was wearing a neat gray pantsuit with a white blouse, her hair was up in a French twist, and she lifted her chin to show that she wasn't afraid of them. Feeling her chances of a physical defense waning rapidly as she saw the size and strength of the two men, her hand went nervously to the whistle in her pocketbook and brought it by her side.

"Hey, there, sweet thing," one of the men called. "Got a flat? We'll help you change it."

The other man, a little taller, untidy, unshaved and frankly unpleasant-looking, grinned at her. "You bet we will!"

"I don't have a spare, thank you all the same."

"We'll drive you home," the tall one said.

She forced a smile. "No, thanks. I'll enjoy the walk. Good night!"

She started to turn when they pounced. One knocked the whistle out of her hand and caught her arm behind her back, while the other one took her purse off her shoulder and went through it quickly. He pulled out her wallet, looked at everything in it, and finally took out a bill, dropping her self-defense spray with the purse.

"Ten lousy bucks," he muttered, dropping the bag as he stuffed the bill into his pocket. "Pity Lopez don't pay us better. This'll buy us a couple of six-packs, though."

"Let me go," Sally said, incensed. She tried to bring her elbow back into the man's stomach, as she'd seen an instructor on television do, but the man twisted her other arm so harshly that the pain stopped her dead.

The other man came right up to her and looked her up and down. "Not bad," he rasped. "Quick, bring her over here, off the road," he told the other man.

"Lopez won't like this!" The man on the porch came toward them, yelling across the road. "You'll draw attention to us!"

One of them made a rude remark. The third man went back up on the porch, his footsteps sounding unnaturally loud on the wood.

Sally was almost sick with fear, but she fought like a

tigress. Her efforts to break free did no good. These men were bigger and stronger than she was, and they had her helpless. She couldn't get to her whistle or spray and every kick, punch she tried was effectively blocked. It occurred to her that these men knew self-defense moves, too, and how to avoid them. Too late, she remembered what Eb had said to her about overconfidence. These men weren't even drunk and they were too much for her.

Her heart beat wildly as she was dragged off the road to the thick grass at the roadside. She would struggle, she would fight, but she was no match for them. She knew she was in a lot of danger and it looked like there was no escape. Tears of impotent fury dripped from her eyes. Helpless while one of the men kept her immobilized, she remembered the sound of her own voice telling her aunt just a few weeks ago that she could handle anything. She'd been overconfident.

A sound buzzed in her head and at first she thought it was the prelude to a dead faint. It wasn't. The sound was growing closer. It was a pickup truck. The headlights illuminated her truck on the roadside, but not the struggle that was going on near it.

It was as if the driver knew what was happening without seeing it. The truck whipped onto the shoulder and was cut off. A man got out, a tall man in a shepherd's coat with a Stetson drawn over his brow. He walked straight toward the two men, who released Jessica and turned to face the new threat. Eb!

"Car trouble?" a deep, gravelly voice asked sarcastically.

One of the men pulled a knife, and the other one approached the newcomer. "This ain't none of your business," the taller man said. "Get going."

The newcomer put his hands on his lean hips and stood his ground. "In your dreams."

"You'll wish you had," the taller of them replied harshly. He moved in with the knife close in at his side.

Sally stared in horror at Eb, who was inviting this lunatic to kill him! She knew from television how deadly a knife wound in the stomach could be. Hadn't Eb told her that the best way to survive a knife fight was to never get in one in the first place, to run like hell? And now Eb was going to be killed and it was going to be all her fault for not taking his advice and getting that tire fixed...!

Eb moved unexpectedly, with the speed of a striking cobra. The man with the knife was suddenly writhing on the ground, holding his forearm and sobbing. The other man rushed forward, to be flipped right out into the highway. He got up and rushed again. This time he was met with a violent, sharp movement that sent him to the ground, and he didn't get up.

Eb walked right over the unconscious man, ignoring the groaning man, and picked Sally up right off the ground in his arms. He carried her to his truck, balancing her on one powerful denim-covered thigh while he opened the passenger door and put her inside.

"My...purse," she whispered, giving in to the shock and fear that she'd tried so hard to hide. She was shaking so hard her speech was slurred.

He closed the door, retrieved her purse and wallet from the ground, and handed it in through his open door. "What did they take, baby?" he asked in a soft, comforting tone.

"The tall one...took a ten-dollar bill," she faltered, hating her own cowardice as she sobbed helplessly. "In his pocket..."

Eb retrieved it, tossed it to her and got in beside her.

"But those men," she protested.

"Be still for a minute. It's all right. They look worse than they are." He took a cell phone from his pocket, opened it, and dialed. "Bill? Eb Scott. I left you a couple of assailants on the Simmons Mill Road just past Bell's rental house. That's right, the very one." He glanced at Sally. "Not tonight. I'll tell her to come see you in the morning." There was a pause. "Nothing too bad; a couple of broken bones, that's all, but you might send the ambulance anyway. Sure. Thanks, Bill."

He powered down the phone and stuck it back into his jacket. "Fasten your seat belt. I'll take you home and send one of my men out to fix the truck and drive it back for you."

Her hands were shaking so badly that he had to do it for her. He turned on the light in the cab and looked at her intently. He saw the shock, the fear, the humiliation, the anger, all lying naked in her wide, shimmering gray eyes. Last, his eyes fell to her blouse, where the fabric was torn, and her simple cotton brassiere was showing. She was so upset that she didn't even realize how much bare skin was on display.

He took off the long-sleeved chambray shirt he was wearing over his black T-shirt and put her into it, fastening the buttons with deft, quick hands over the ripped blouse. His face grew hard as he saw the evidence of her ordeal.

"I had a...a...whistle." she choked. "I even remembered what you taught me about how to fight back...!"

He studied her solemnly. "I trained a company of recruits a few years ago," he said evenly. "They'd had hand-to-hand combat training and they knew all the right moves to counter any sort of physical attack. There wasn't one of them that I couldn't drop in less than ten seconds." His pale green eyes searched hers. "Even a martial artist can lose a match. It depends on the skill of his opponent and his ability to keep his head when the attack comes. I've seen karate instructors send advanced students running with nothing more dangerous than the yell, a sudden quick sound that paralyzes.''

"Those two men…they couldn't…touch you," she pointed out, amazed.

His pale eyes had an alien coldness that made her shiver. "I told you to get that damned tire fixed, Sally."

She swallowed. Her pride was bruised almost beyond bearing. "I don't take orders," she said, trying to salvage a little self-respect.

"I don't give them anymore," he returned. "But I do give advice, and you've just seen the results of not listening. At least you had the sense to leave a message on my answering machine. But what if I hadn't checked my messages, Sally? Would you like to think where you'd be now? Want me to paint you a picture?"

"Stop!" She put her face in her hands and shivered.

"I won't apologize," he told her abruptly. "You did a damned stupid thing and you got off lucky. Another time, I might not be quick enough."

She swallowed and swallowed again. "The…conquering male," she choked, but she wasn't teasing now, as she had been that afternoon when he'd told her to get the tire fixed.

He drew her hands away from her face and looked into her eyes steadily. "That's right," he said curtly, and he wasn't kidding. "I've been dealing with vermin like that for almost half my life. I told you there was danger in going out alone. Now you understand what I meant. Get that damned tire fixed, and buy a cell phone."

Her head was spinning. "I can't afford one," she said unsteadily.

"You can't afford not to. If you'd had one tonight, this

might never have happened," he said forcefully. The heat in his eyes made her shiver. "A man is physically stronger than a woman. There are some exceptions, but for the most part, that's the honest truth. Unless you've trained for years, like a policewoman or a federal agent, you're not going to be the equal of a man who's drunk or on drugs or just bent on assault. Law enforcement people know how to fight. You don't."

She shivered again. Her hair was disheveled. She felt bruises on her arms where she'd been restrained by those men. She was still stunned by the experience, but already a little of the horror of what might have happened was getting to her.

He let her wrists go abruptly. His lean face softened as he studied her. "But I'll say one thing for you. You've got grit."

"Sure. I'm tough," she laughed hollowly, brushing a strand of loose hair out of her eyes. "What a pitiful waste of self-confidence!"

"Who the hell taught you about canned self-defense?" he asked curiously, referring to the can of spray on the ground.

"There was this television self-defense training course for women," she said defensively.

"Anything you spray, pepper or chemical, can rebound on you," he said quietly. "If the wind's blowing the wrong way, you can blind yourself. If you don't hit the attacker squarely in the eyes, you're no better off, either. As for the whistle, tonight there would have been no one close enough to hear it." He sighed at her miserable expression and shook his head. "Didn't I tell you to run?"

She lifted a high-heeled foot eloquently.

He leaned closer. "If you're ever in a similar situation again, kick them off and try for the two-minute mile!"

She managed a smile for him. "Okay."

He touched her wan, drawn face gently. "I wouldn't have had that happen to you for the world," he said bitterly.

"You were right, I brought it on myself. I won't make that mistake again, and at least I got away with everything except my pride intact," she said gamely.

He unfastened her seat belt, aware of a curtain being lifted and then released in the living room. "I sent Dallas straight here as soon as I got the message," he explained, "to watch out for Jess and Stevie. You should have let me know about this night meeting much sooner."

"I know." She was fighting tears. The whole experience had been a shock that she knew she'd never get over. "There was a third man, on the porch. He said that Lopez wouldn't like what they were doing, calling attention to themselves."

He stared at her for a long moment, seeing the fear and terror and revulsion that lingered in her oval face, watching the way her hands clenched at the shirt he'd fastened over her torn bodice. He glanced at the window, where the curtain was in place again, and back to Sally's face.

"Come here, sweetheart," he said tenderly, pulling her into his arms. He cuddled her close, nuzzling his face into her throat, letting her cry.

Her clenched fist rested against his black undershirt and she sobbed with impotent fury. "Oh, I'm so...mad!" she choked. "So mad! I felt like a rag doll."

"You do your best and take what comes," he said at her ear. "Anybody can lose a fight."

"I'll bet you never lost one," she muttered tearfully.

"I got the hell beaten out of me in boot camp by a little guy half my size, who was a hapkido master. Taught me a valuable lesson about overconfidence," he said deliberately.

She took the handkerchief he placed in her hands and wiped her nose and eyes and mouth. "Okay, I get the message," she said on a broken sigh. "There's always somebody bigger and you can't win every time."

"Nice attitude," he said, approving.

She wiped away the last trace of tears and looked up at him from her comfortable position across his lap. "Thanks for the hero stuff."

He shrugged. "Shucks, ma'am, t'weren't nothin'."

She laughed, as she was meant to. Her eyes adored him. "They say that if you save a life, it becomes yours."

His lips pursed and he looked down at where the jacket barely covered her torn blouse. "Do I get that, too?"

"Too?"

He opened the shirt very slowly and looked at the pale flesh under the torn blouse. There was a lot of it on view. Sally didn't protest, didn't grab at cover. She lay very still in his arms and let him look at her.

His pale eyes met hers in the faint light coming from the house. "No protest?"

"You saved me," she said simply. She sighed and smiled with resignation. "I belonged to you, anyway. There's never been anyone else."

His long, lean fingers touched her collarbone, his eyes narrow and solemn, his expression serious, intent. "That could have changed, tonight," he reminded her quietly. "You have to trust me enough to do what I tell you. I don't want you hurt in this. I'll do anything I have to, to protect you. That includes having a man follow you around like a visible appendage if you push me to it. Think what your principal would make of *that!*"

"I won't make any more stupid mistakes," she promised.

"What would you call this?" he mused, nodding toward the ripped fabric that left one pretty, taut breast completely bare.

"Cover me up if you don't like what you see," she challenged.

He actually laughed. She was constantly surprising him. "I think I'd better," he murmured dryly, and pulled the shirt back over her, leaving her to button it again. "Dallas is at the window getting an education."

"And I can tell how much he needs it," she said with dry humor as Eb helped her back into her own seat.

"That makes two of you," Eb told her. His eyes were kind, and now full of concern. "Will you be all right?"

"Yes." She hesitated with her hand on the doorknob. "Eb, is it always like that?"

He frowned. "What?"

She looked up into his eyes. "Physical violence. Do you ever get to the point that it doesn't make you sick inside?"

"I never have," he said flatly. "I remember every face, every sound, every sick minute of what I've done in my life." He looked at her, but he seemed to go far away. "You'd better go inside. I'll take you and Stevie out to the ranch Thursday and Saturday and we'll put in some more time."

"For all the good it will do me," she managed to say nervously.

"Don't be like that," he chided. "You got overpowered. People do, even 'big, strong' men. There's no shame in losing a fight when you've given it all you've got."

She smiled. "Think so?"

"I know so." He touched her disheveled French knot. "You wore your hair down that spring afternoon," he murmured softly. "I remember how it felt on my bare chest, loose and smelling of flowers."

Her breath seemed to stick in her throat as she recalled the same memory. They had both been bare to the waist. She could close her eyes and feel the hair-roughened muscles of his chest against her own softness as he kissed her and kissed her…

"Sometimes," he continued, "we get second chances."

"Do we?" she whispered.

He touched her mouth gently. "Try not to dwell on what happened tonight," he said. "I won't let anyone hurt you, Sally."

That felt nice. She wished she could give him the same guarantee, but it seemed pretty ridiculous after her poor performance.

He seemed to read the thought right in her mind, and he burst out laughing. "Listen, lady, when I get through with you, you'll be eating bad men raw," he promised. "You're just a beginner."

"You aren't."

"That's true. And not only in self-defense," he added dryly. "You'd better go in."

"I suppose so." She picked at the buttons of the shirt he'd loaned her. "I'll give it back. Eventually."

"You look nice in it," he had to admit. "You can keep it. We'll try some more of my clothes on you and see how they look."

She made a face at him as she opened the door. "Eb, do I have to go and see the sheriff?"

"You do. I'll pick you up after school. Don't worry," he said quietly. "He won't eat you. He's a nice man. But you must see that we can't let Lopez's people get away with this."

She felt a chill go down her arms as she remembered

who Lopez was. "What will he do if I testify against his men?"

"You let me worry about that," Eb told her, and his eyes were like green steel. "Nobody touches you without going through me."

Her heart jumped right up into her throat as she stared at him. She was a modern woman, and she probably shouldn't have enjoyed that passionate remark. But she did. Eb was a strong, assertive man who would want a woman to match him. Sally hadn't been that woman at seventeen. But she was now. She could stand up to him and meet him on his own ground. It gave her a sense of pride.

"Debating if it's proper for a modern woman to like being protected?" he chided with a wicked grin.

"You said yourself that none of us are invincible," she pointed out. "I don't think it's a bad thing to admire a man's strength, especially when it's just saved my neck."

He made her feel confident, he gave her joy. It had been years since she'd laughed so much, enjoyed life so much. Odd that a man whose adult years had been imbued with such violence could be so tender.

"Okay now?" he asked.

She nodded. "I'm okay." She glanced toward the road and shivered a little. "They won't come looking for me?"

"Not in that condition they won't," he said matter-of-factly. "And they're very lucky," he added, his whole face like drawn cord. "Ten years ago, I wouldn't have been so gentle."

Both eyebrows went up at the imagery.

"You know what I was," he said quietly. "Until comparatively recent years, I lived a violent, uncertain life. Part of the man I was is still in me. I won't ever hurt you," he added. "But I have to come to grips with the old life before I can begin a new one. That's going to take time."

"I think you're saying something."

"Why, yes, I am," he mused, watching her. "I'm giving notice of my intentions."

"Intentions?"

"Last time I stopped. Next time I won't."

Her mind wasn't quite grasping what he was telling her. "You mean, with those men...?"

"I mean with you," he said gently. "I want you very badly, and I'm not walking away this time."

"You and what army?" she asked, aghast.

"I won't need an army. But you might." He smiled. "Go on in. I'm having the house watched. You'll be safe, I promise."

She pulled his shirt closer. "Thanks, Eb," she said.

He shrugged. "I have to take care of my own. Try to sleep."

She smiled at him. "Okay. You, too."

He watched her go up onto the porch and into the house, waiting for Dallas, who came out tight-lipped with barely a word to Sally as he passed her.

He got into the truck with Eb and slammed the door.

"What happened to Sally?" he asked, putting his cane aside.

"Lopez's men rushed the truck when she had a flat. I don't know if it was premeditated," he added coldly. "They could have lain in wait for her and caused the flat. The tire was almost bald, but it could have gone another few hundred miles."

"She looked uneasy."

"They assaulted her and may have raped her if I hadn't shown up," Eb said bluntly as he backed the truck and pulled out into the road. "I want to have another look, if the ambulance hasn't picked them up yet."

"You sent for an ambulance?" Dallas asked with mock surprise. "That's new."

"Well, we're trying to blend in, aren't we?" came the terse reply. He glared at the tall blond man. "Difficult to blend in if we let people die on the side of the road."

"If you say so."

They drove to where Sally's pickup truck was still sitting, but there was no sign of the two men. The house nearby was dark. There wasn't a soul in sight.

As Eb digested that, red lights flashed and a big boxy ambulance pulled up behind the pickup truck, followed closely by a deputy sheriff in a patrol car.

Eb pulled off the road and got out. He knew the deputy, Rich Burton, who was one of the department's ablest members. They shook hands.

"Where are the victims?" Rich asked.

Eb grimaced. "Well, they were both lying right there when I took Sally home."

The deputy and the ambulance guys looked toward the flattened grass, but there weren't any men lying there.

"Unless one of you needs medical attention, we'll be on our way," one of the EMTs said with a wry glance.

"Both of the perps did," Eb said quietly. "At least one of them has broken bones."

The EMT gave him a wary look. "Not their legs, by the look of things."

"No. Not their legs."

The EMTs left and Rich joined Eb and Dallas beside the truck.

"Something's going on at that house," Rich said quietly. "I've had total strangers stop me and tell me they've seen suspicious activity, men carrying boxes in and out.

That's not all. Some holding company bought a huge tract of land adjoining Cy Parks's place, and it's filling up with building supplies. There's a contractor been hired and a plan has gone to the county commission's planning committee about a business starting up there.''

''How much do you know about the men who live here?'' Eb asked coolly.

Rich shrugged. ''Not as much as I'd like to. But my contacts tell me that there's a drug lord named Manuel Lopez, and the talk is that these guys belong to him. They're mules. They run his narcotics for him.''

Eb and Dallas exchanged quiet glances.

''What sort of business are we talking about?'' Eb queried.

''Don't know. There's a huge steel warehouse going up behind Parks's place,'' Rich replied, and he looked worried. ''If I were making a guess, and it is just a guess, I'd say somebody had distribution in mind.''

Chapter Five

"A distribution center," Eb said curtly. "With Manuel Lopez, the head of the most violent of the international drug cartels, behind it! That's just what we need in Jacobsville."

"That's right," the younger man replied. He scowled. "How do you know about Lopez?"

Eb didn't answer. "Thanks, Rich," he said. "If I hear anything about the men who attacked Miss Johnson, I'll give you a call."

"Thanks. But I'd bet that they're long gone," he said carelessly. "They'd be crazy to stick around and face charges like attempted rape in a town this size. Lopez wouldn't like the notoriety."

"My guess exactly. So long," Eb said, motioning to Dallas. Rich drove off with a wave of his hand. Eb hesitated, and once Rich was out of sight, he looked for and found a board with new nails sticking through it. It was lying point-side down, now, but the wood was new and there was a long cord attached to it. Evidently it had been placed in the road just as Sally approached, and then jerked away once Sally had run over it. That meant that there had to be a fourth man involved, besides the man on the porch and the two men who'd assaulted Sally. That disturbed Eb.

"They set a trap," Dallas guessed. "She ran over this. That's how she got the flat."

"Exactly." Eb threw the board in the bed of the truck before he climbed in under the wheel. "There were at least four men in on it, and I don't think assault was the sole object of the exercise. I think I'll go over and have a talk with Cy Parks first thing in the morning. He may know something about that new construction behind his place."

Cy Parks was grumpy. He hadn't been able to sleep the night before, and he was groggy. Even after four years, he still had nightmares about the loss of his wife and five-year-old son in a fire back home in Wyoming. He'd moved here to Jacobsville, where Ebenezer Scott lived, more for someone to talk to than any other reason. Eb was not only a former comrade at arms, but he was also the only man he knew who could listen to the unabridged horror of the fire without losing his supper. It kept him sane, just having someone to talk to. And not only could he talk about the death of his family at Lopez's henchmen's hands but also he had someone to help him exorcise the nightmares of the past that he and Ebenezer shared.

The knock on the door came just as he was pouring his second cup of coffee. It was probably his foreman. Harley Fowler was an adventurer wanna-be who fancied himself a mercenary. He was forever reading a magazine for armchair adventurers and once he'd actually answered one of the ads for volunteers and, supposedly, had taken a job during his summer vacation. He'd come back from his vacation two weeks later grinning and bragging about his exploits overseas with a group of world-beaters and lording it over the other ranch hands who worked for Cy. Harley had become the overnight hero of the men. Cy watched him with amused cynicism. None of the men he'd served with had ever returned home strutting and bragging about their exploits. Nor had any of them come home smiling. There was a look about a man who'd seen combat. It was unmistakable to anyone who'd been through it. Harley didn't have the look.

None of the ranch hands knew that Cy Parks hadn't always been a rancher. They knew about the fire that had cost him his family—most people locally did. But they didn't know that he was a former professional mercenary and that Lopez was responsible for the fire. Cy wanted to keep it that way. He was through with the old life.

He opened the front door with a scowl on his lean, tanned face, but it wasn't Harley who was standing on his porch. It was Ebenezer Scott.

Cy's eyes, two shades darker green than Eb's, narrowed. "Lost your way?" he taunted, running a hand through his thick unruly black hair.

Eb chuckled. "Years ago. Got another cup?"

"Sure." He opened the door and let Eb in. The living room, old-fashioned and sparsely furnished, was neat as a pin. So were the formal dining room—never used—and the big, airy kitchen with not a spot of dirt or grime anywhere.

"Tell me you hired a housekeeper," Eb murmured.

Cy got down an extra cup and poured black coffee into it, handing it across the table before he sat down. "I don't need a housekeeper," he replied. "Why are you here?" he added with characteristic bluntness.

"Did you keep in touch with any of your old contacts when you got out of the business?" Eb asked at once.

Cy shook his head. "No need. I gave it up, remember?" He lifted the cup to his wide, chiseled mouth.

Eb sipped coffee, nodded at the strength of it, and put the mug down on the Formica tabletop with a soft thud. "Manuel Lopez is loose," he said without preamble. "We think he's in the vicinity. Certainly some of his henchmen are."

Cy's face hardened. "Are you certain?"

"Yes."

"Why is he here?"

"Because Jessica Myers is here," Eb replied. "She's living with her young son and her niece, Sally Johnson, out at the old Johnson place. She got one of Lopez's accomplices to rat on Lopez without giving himself away. She had access to documents and bank accounts and witnesses willing to testify. Now Lopez is out and he's after Jess. He wants the name of the henchman who sold him out."

Cy made an impatient gesture. "Fighting out in the open isn't Lopez's style. He's the original knife-in-the-back boy."

"I know. It worries me." He sipped more coffee. "He had three, maybe four, of his thugs living in a rental place near Sally's house. Two of them attacked her last night when her truck had a flat tire just down the road from them. It was no accident, either. They've obviously been gathering intelligence, watching her. They knew exactly where she was and exactly when she'd get as far as their place." His face was grim. "I think there are more than four of them. I also think they may have the same sort of surveillance equipment I maintain at the ranch. What I don't know is why. I don't know if it's solely because Lopez wants to get to Jessica."

"Is Sally all right?"

Eb nodded. "I got to her in time, luckily. I broke a

couple of bones for her assailants, but they got away and now the house seems to be without tenants—temporarily, of course. Have you noticed any activity on your northern boundary?"

"As a matter of fact, I have," Cy replied, frowning. "All sorts of vehicles are coming and going. They've graded about an acre, and a steel warehouse is going up. The city planning commission chairman says it's going to be some sort of production and distribution center for a honey concern. They even have a building permit." He sighed angrily. "Matt Caldwell has been having hell with the planning commission about a project of his own, yet this gang got what they wanted immediately."

"Honey," Eb mused.

"That isn't all of it," Cy continued. "I investigated the holding company that bought the land behind me. It doesn't belong to anybody local, but I can't find out who's behind it. It belongs to a corporation based in Cancún, Mexico."

Eb's eyes narrowed. "Cancún? Now, that's interesting. The last report I had about Lopez before he was arrested was that he bought property there and was living like a king in a palatial estate just outside Cancún." He stopped dead at the expression on his friend's face. Cy and Eb had once helped put some of Lopez's men away.

Cy's breathing became rough, his green eyes began to glitter like heated emeralds. "Lopez! Now what the hell would he want with a honey business?"

"It's evidently going to be a front for something illegal," Eb assured him. "He may have picked Jacobsville for a distribution center for his 'product' because it's small, isolated, and there are no federal agencies represented near here."

Cy stood up, his whole body rigid with hatred and anger. "He killed my wife and son...!"

"He had Jessica run off the road and almost killed," Eb added coldly. "She lived, but she was blinded. She came back here from Houston, hoping that I could protect her. But it's going to take more than me. I need help. I want to set up a listening post on your back forty and put a man there."

"Done," Cy said at once. "But first I'm going to buy a few claymores..."

It took a minute for the expression on Cy's face, in his eyes, in the set of his lean body to register. Eb had only seen him like that once before, in combat, many years before. Probably that was the way he'd looked when his wife and son died and he was hospitalized with severe burns on one arm, incurred when he'd tried to save them from the raging fire. He hadn't known at the time that Lopez had sent men to kill him. Even in prison, Lopez could put out contracts.

"You can't start setting off land mines. You have to think with your brain, not your guts," Eb said curtly. "If we're going to get Lopez, we have to do it legally."

"Oh, that's new, coming from you," Cy said with biting sarcasm.

Eb's broad shoulders lifted and fell as he sat down again, straddling the chair this time. "I'm reformed," he said. "I want to settle down, but first I have to put Lopez away. I need you."

Cy extended the hand that had been so badly burned.

"I know about the burns," Eb said. "If you recall, most of us went to see you in the hospital afterward."

Cy averted his eyes and pulled the sleeve down over his wrist, holding it there protectively. "I don't remember much of it," he confessed. "They sent me to a burn unit and did what they could. At least I was able to keep the arm, but I'll never be much good in a tight corner again."

"You mean you were before?" Eb asked with howling mockery.

Cy's eyes widened, narrowed and suddenly he burst out laughing. "I'd forgotten what a bunch of sadists you and your men were," he accused. "Before every search and destroy mission, somebody was claiming my gear and asking about my beneficiary." Cy drew in a long breath. "I've been keeping to myself for a long time."

"So we noticed," came the dry reply. "I hear it took a bunch of troubled adolescents to drag you out of your cave."

Cy knew what he meant. Belinda Jessup, a public defender, had bought some of the property on his boundary for a summer camp for youthful offenders on probation. One of the boys, an African-American youth who'd fallen absolutely in love with the cattle business, had gotten through his shell. He'd worked with Luke Craig, another neighbor, to give the boy a head start in cowboying. He was now working for Luke Craig on his ranch and had made a top hand. No more legal troubles for him. He was on his way to being foreman of the whole outfit, and Cy couldn't repress a tingle of pride that he'd had a hand in that.

"Even assuming that we can send Lopez back to prison, that won't stop him from appointing somebody to run his empire. You know how these groups are organized," Cy added, "into cells of ten or more men with their chiefs reporting to a regional manager and those managers reporting to a high-level management designee. The damned cartels operate on a corporate structure these days."

"Yes, I know, and they work complete with pagers, cell phones and faxes, using them just long enough to avoid detection," Eb agreed. "They're efficient and they're merciless. God only knows how many undercover agents the drug enforcement people have lost, not to mention those from other law enforcement agencies. The drug lords make a religion of intimidation, and they have no scruples about killing a man and his entire family. No wonder few of their henchmen ever cross them. But one did, and Jessica knows his name. I don't expect Lopez to give up. Ever."

"Neither do I. But what are we going to do about Lopez's planned operation?" Cy wanted to know.

Eb sobered. "I don't have a plan yet. Legally, we can't do anything without hard evidence. Lopez will be extra careful about covering his tracks this time. He won't want anything that will connect him on paper to the drug operation. From what I've been able to learn, Lopez has already skipped town, forfeiting the bond. Believe me, there's no way in hell he'll ever get extradited from Mexico. The only way we'll ever get him back behind bars again is to lure him back here and have him nabbed by the U.S. Marshals Service. He's at the top of the DEA's Most Wanted list right now." He finished his second cup of coffee. "If we can get a legal wiretap on the phones in that warehouse once it's operating, we might have something to take to the authorities. I know a DEA agent," Eb said thoughtfully. "In fact, he and his wife are neighbors of yours. He's gung-ho at his job, and he's done some undercover work before."

"Most of Lopez's people are Hispanic," Cy pointed out.

"This guy could pass for Hispanic. Good-looking devil, too. His wife's father left her that small ranch..."

"Lisa Monroe," Cy said, and averted his eyes. "Yes, I've seen her around. Yesterday she was heaving bales of hay over the fence to her horse," he added in the coldest tones Eb had ever heard him use. "She's thinner than she should be, and she has no business trying to heft bales of hay!"

"When her husband's not home to do it for her…"

"Not home?" Cy's eyes widened. "Good God, man, he was standing ten feet away talking to a leggy blond girl in an express delivery uniform! He didn't even seem to notice Lisa!"

"It's not our business."

Cy moved abruptly, standing up. "Okay. Point taken. Suppose we ride up to the boundary and take a look at the progress on that warehouse," he said. "We can take horses and pretend we're riding the fence line."

Eb retrieved high-powered binoculars from the truck and by the time he got to the stable, Cy's young foreman had two horses saddled and waiting.

"Mr. Scott!" Harley said with a starstruck grin, running an absent hand through his crew-cut light brown hair. "Nice to see you, sir!" He almost saluted. He knew about Mr. Scott's operation; he'd read all about it in his armchair covert operations magazine, to say nothing of the top secret newsletter to which he subscribed.

Eb gave him a measuring glance and he didn't smile. "Do I know you, son?"

"Oh, no, sir," Harley said quickly. "But I've read about your operation!"

"I can imagine what," Eb chuckled. He stuck a cigar into his mouth and lit it.

Cy mounted offside, from the right, because there wasn't enough strength in his left arm to permit him to grip the saddle horn and help pull himself up. He hated the show of weakness, which was all too visible. Up until the fire, he'd been in superb physical condition.

"We're going to ride up to the northern boundary and

check the fence line for breaks,'' Cy said imperturbably.
"Get Jenkins started on the new gate as soon as he's
through with breakfast.''

"He'll have to go pick it up at the hardware store first,"
Harley reminded him. "Just came in late yesterday."

Cy gave him a look that would have frozen running
water. He didn't say anything. But, then, he didn't have
to.

"I'll just go remind him," Harley said at once, and took
off toward the bunkhouse.

"Who is he?" Eb asked as they rode out of the yard.

"My new foreman." Cy leaned toward him with mock
awe. "He's a real *mercenary,* you know! Actually went
on a mission early this summer!"

"My God," Eb drawled. "Fancy that. A real live hero
right here in the boonies."

"Some hero," Cy muttered. "Chances are what he really did was to camp out in the woods for two weeks and
help protect city campers from bears."

Eb chuckled. "Remember how we were at his age?" he
asked reminiscently. "We couldn't wait for people to see
us in our gear. And then we found out that the real mercs
don't advertise."

"We were like Harley," Cy mused. "All talk and hot
air."

"And all smiles." Eb's eyes narrowed with memory. "I
hadn't smiled for years by the time I got out. It isn't ro-
mantic and no matter how good the pay is, it's never
enough for what you have to do for it."

"We did do a little good in the world," came the re-
joinder.

"Yes, I guess we did," Eb had to admit. "But our best
job was breaking up one of Lopez's cocaine processing

plants in Central America and helping put Lopez away. And here he is back, like a bad bouncing ball.''

"I knew his father," Cy said unexpectedly. "A good, honest, bighearted man who worked as a janitor just up the road in Victoria and studied English at home every night trying to better himself. He died just after he found out what his only child was doing for a living."

Eb stared off into space. "You never know how kids will turn out."

"I know how mine would have turned out," Cy said heavily. "One of his teachers was in an accident. Not a well-liked teacher, but Alex started a fund for him and gave up a whole month's allowance to start it with." His face corded like wire. He had to swallow, hard, to keep his voice from breaking. The years hadn't made his memories any easier. Perhaps if he could help get Lopez back in prison, it might help.

"We'll get Lopez," the other man said abruptly. "Whatever it takes, if I have to call in markers from all over the world. We'll get him."

Cy came out of his brief torment and glanced at his comrade. "If we do, I get five minutes alone with him."

"Not a chance," Eb said with a grin. "I remember what you can do in five minutes, and I want him tried properly."

"He already was."

"Yes, but he was caught and tried back east. This time we'll manage to apprehend him right here in Texas and we'll stack the legal deck by having the best prosecuting attorney in the state brought in to do the job. The Hart boys are related to the state attorney general—he's their big brother."

"I'd forgotten." He glanced at Eb. His eyes were briefly less tormented. "Okay. I guess I can give the court a second chance. Not their fault that Lopez can afford defense attorneys in Armani suits, I guess.''

"Absolutely. And if we can catch him with enough laundered money in his pockets and invoke the RICO statutes, we can fund some nice improvements for our drug enforcement people.''

They'd arrived at the northernmost boundary of Cy's property, and barely in sight across the high-wire fence was a huge construction site. From their concealed position in a small stand of trees near a stream, Eb took his binoculars and gave the area a thorough scrutiny. He handed them to Cy, who looked as well and then handed them back.

"Recognize anybody?'' Cy asked.

Eb shook his head. "None of them are familiar. But I'll bet if you looked in the right places, you could find a rap sheet or two. Lopez isn't too picky about pedigrees. He just likes men who don't mind doing whatever the job takes. Last I heard, he had several foreign nationals in his employ.'' He sighed. "I sure as hell don't want a drug distribution network out here.''

"Neither do I. We'd better go have a word with Bill Elliott at the sheriff's office.''

Cy shrugged. "You'd better have a word with him by yourself, if you want to get anywhere. I'd jinx you.''

"I remember now. You had words with him over Belinda Jessup's summer camp.''

"Hard words,'' Cy agreed uncomfortably. "I've mellowed since, though.''

"You and the KGB.'' He pulled his hat further over his eyes. "We'd better get out of here before they spot us.''

"I can see people coming.''

"They can see you coming, too.''

"That should worry them,'' Cy agreed, grinning.

Eb chuckled. It was rare these days to see a smile on that hard face. He wheeled his horse, leaving Cy to follow.

That afternoon, Eb drove over to the Johnson place to pick up Sally and Stevie for their self-defense practice.

Sally's eyes lit up when she saw him and he felt his heart jump. She made him feel warm inside, as if he finally belonged somewhere. Stevie ran past his aunt to be caught up and swung around in Eb's muscular arms.

"How's Jess?" Eb asked.

Sally made a face and glanced back toward the house. "Dallas got here just before you did. It's sort of unarmed combat in there. They aren't even speaking to each other."

"Ah, well," he mused. "Things will improve eventually."

"Do you gamble?" she teased. "I feel a lucky streak coming on."

He chuckled as he loaded them into the pickup. No, he wasn't willing to bet on friendlier relations on that front. Not yet, anyway.

"How much do you know about surveillance equipment?" Sally asked unexpectedly.

He gave her a look of exaggerated patience. "With my background, how much do you think I know?"

She laughed. "Sorry. I wasn't thinking. Can a microphone really pick up voices inside the house? Jess tried to convince me that they could hear us through the walls and we had to be very careful what we discussed. I mentioned that Lopez man and she shushed me immediately."

He glanced at her as he drove. "You've got a lot to learn. I suppose now is as good a time as any to teach you."

When he parked the truck at the front door, he led her inside, parking Stevie at the kitchen table with Carl, his cook, who dished up some ice cream for the child while Eb led Sally down the long hall and into a huge room literally crammed with electronic equipment.

He motioned her into a chair and keyed his security camera to a distant view of two cowboys working on a piece of machinery halfway down a rutted path in the meadow.

He flipped a switch and she heard one cowboy muttering to the other about the sorry state of modern tools and how even rusted files were better than what passed for a file today.

They weren't even talking loud, and if there was a microphone, it must be mounted on the barn wall outside. She looked at Eb with wide, frankly disbelieving eyes.

He flipped the switch and the screen was silent again. "Most modern sound equipment can pick up a whisper several hundred yards away." He indicated a shelf upon which sat several pair of odd-looking binoculars. "Night vision. I can see anything on a moonless night with those, and I've got others that detect heat patterns in the dark."

"You have got to be kidding!"

"We have cameras hidden in books and cigarette packs, we have weapons that can be broken down and hidden in boots," he continued. "Not to mention this."

He indicated his watch, a quite normal looking one with all sorts of dials. Normal until he adjusted it and a nasty-looking little blade popped out. Her gasp was audible.

He could see the realization in her eyes as the purpose of the blade registered there. She looked up at him and saw the past. His past.

His green eyes narrowed as they searched hers. "You hadn't really thought about exactly what sort of work I did, had you?"

She shook her head. She was a little paler now.

"I lived in dangerous places, in dangerous times. It's only in recent years that I've stopped looking over my shoulder and sitting with my back against a wall." He touched her face. "Lopez's men can hear you through a wall, with the television on. Don't ever forget. Say nothing that you don't want recorded for posterity."

"This Lopez man is very dangerous, isn't he?" she asked.

"He's the most dangerous man I know. He hires killers. He has no compassion, no mercy, and he'll do absolutely anything for profit. If his henchman hadn't sold him out, he'd never have been taken into custody in this country. It was a fluke."

She looked around her curiously. "Could he overhear you in here?"

He smiled gently. "Not a chance in hell."

"It looks like something out of *Star Wars*," she mused.

He grinned. "Speaking of movies, how would you and Stevie like to go see a new science fiction flick with me Saturday?"

"Could we?" she asked.

"Sure." His eyes danced wickedly at the idea of sitting in a darkened theater with her....

Chapter Six

Sally found the workouts easier to do as they progressed from falls to defensive moves. Not only was it exciting to learn such skills, but the constant physical contact with Eb was delightful. She couldn't really hide that from him. He saw right through her diversionary tactics, grinning when she asked for short breaks.

Stevie was also taking to the exercise with enthusiasm. It wasn't hard to teach him that such things had no place at school, either. Even at his young age, he seemed to understand that martial arts were for recreation after school and never for the playground.

"It goes with the discipline," Eb informed her when she told him about it. "Most people who watch martial arts films automatically assume that we teach children to hurt each other. It's not like that. What we teach is a way to raise self-esteem and self-confidence. If you know you can handle yourself in a bad situation, you're less likely to go out and try to beat somebody up to prove it. It's lack of self-confidence, lack of self-esteem, that drives a lot of kids to violence.''

"That, and a very sad lack of attention by the adults around them,'' Sally said quietly. "It takes two incomes to run a household these days, but it's the kids who are suffering for it. Any gang member will tell you the reason he joined a gang was because he wanted to be part of a family. But how do we change things so that parents can earn a living and still have enough free time to raise their children?''

He put both hands on his narrow hips and studied her closely. "If I could answer that question, I'd run for public office.''

She grinned at him. "I can see you now, mopping the floor with the criminal element on the streets.''

He shrugged. "Piece of cake compared to what I used to do for a living.''

Her pale eyes searched his lean, scarred face while Stevie fell from one side of the mat to another practicing his technique. "I rented one of those old mercenary films and watched it. Do you guys really throw grenades and use rocket launchers?''

A dark, odd look came into his pale eyes. "Among other things,'' he said.

"Such as?'' she prompted.

"High-tech equipment like the stuff you saw in my office. Plastic explosive charges, small arms, whatever we had. But most of what we do now is intelligence-gathering and tactics. And intelligence gathering,'' he told her dryly, "is about as exciting as two-hour-old cereal in milk.''

She was surprised. "I thought it was like war.''

He shrugged. "Only if you get caught gathering intelligence,'' he replied on a laugh. "We were good at what we did.''

"Dallas was one of your guys, wasn't he?"

He nodded. "Dallas, Cy Parks and Callie Kirby's step-brother Micah Steele, among others."

Her mouth fell open. "Cy Parks was a mercenary?!"

His eyebrows levered up. "You didn't notice that he has a hard time interacting with other people?"

"It's hard to miss. But in the condition he's in..."

"I know. That's one reason that he isn't in our line of work anymore. He was one of the group that helped put Lopez's organization away a little over two years ago—so was I. It was Jess who got to the man himself. But Lopez appealed the verdict and only went to prison six months ago. As you can see, he's out now,' he added dryly.

"Two years ago—that was about the time Cy came to Jacobsville," she recalled.

"Yes. After one of Lopez's goons torched his house in Wyoming. The idea was to kill all three of them, not just Cy's wife and child," he added, seeing the horror in her eyes. "But Cy wasn't asleep, as they'd assumed. He got out."

She grimaced. "But why would Lopez burn his house down?"

"That's how he gets even with people who cross him," he said simply. "He doesn't take out just the person responsible, but the whole family, if he can get to it. There have been slaughters like you wouldn't believe down in Mexico when anyone tried to stand against him. He does usually stop short of children, however; his one virtue."

"I never knew people like him existed," she said sorrowfully.

"I wish I could say the same," he told her. "We don't live in a perfect world. That's why I want you to learn how to defend yourself."

"Fat lot of good it would have done me the night I had

the flat tire," she pointed out. "If you hadn't come along when you did..." She shuddered.

"But I did. Don't look back. It's unproductive."

Her soft, worried eyes searched his scarred face quietly.

"What are you thinking?" he asked with a faint smile.

She shrugged. "I was thinking what a false picture I had of you all those years ago," she admitted. "I suppose I was living in a dream world."

"And I was living in a nightmare," he replied. "That unforgettable spring day six years ago, I'd just come home from a bloodbath in Africa, trying to help an incumbent government fight off a military coup by a very nasty native communist general. I lost most of my unit, including several friends, and the incumbent president's office was blown up, with him in it. It wasn't a good time."

She named the country, to his surprise. "We were studying that in a political science class at the time," she said. "I had no idea what you did for a living, or that you were involved. But we all thought it was an idealistic resistance," she added with a smile.

"Idealistic," he agreed. "And very costly, as most ideas are when you try to put them into practice." His eyes were very old as they met hers. "After that, I began to concentrate on intelligence and tactics. War isn't noble. Only the resolution of it is that."

She recalled the fresh scars on his face that day, scars that she'd attributed to ranch work. She studied him with obvious interest, smiling sheepishly when one of his eyebrows levered up.

"Sorry," she murmured.

He moved a step closer to her, forcing her to raise her chin so that she could see his face. The contact, barely perceptible, made her heart race. It wasn't so much the proximity as the way he was looking at her, as if he'd like to press her against him and kiss her until she couldn't stand up.

She moved a step back, her gaze going involuntarily to her cousin, who was giving the punching bag a hard time.

"I hadn't forgotten he was there," Eb said in a velvety tone. His pale eyes fell to her mouth and lingered. Even without makeup and with her long hair disheveled, she was pretty. "One night soon I'm going to take you out to dinner. Dallas can keep an eye on Jess and Stevie while you're away."

Until he said that, she'd actually forgotten the danger for a few delightful minutes. It all came rushing back.

He smoothed out the frown between her thin eyebrows. "Don't brood. I've got everything under control."

"I hope so," she said uneasily. "Does Mr. Parks know that Lopez is out of prison?"

"He knows," Eb replied. He ran a hand through his thick hair. "He's the one loose cannon I'm going to have to watch. Even in the old days, Cy never had much patience. He and his wife weren't much of a pair, but he loved that boy to death. He won't rest until Lopez is caught, and if he gets to him first, we can forget about a trial. You can't ever afford to act in anger," he added quietly. "Anger clouds reason. It can get you killed."

"You can't really blame him for the way he feels. Poor man," she sympathized.

"Pity would be wasted on him," he murmured with a smile. "Even crippled, he's more man than most."

"I don't think of him as crippled," she said genuinely. "He's very attractive."

He glared down at her. "You're off limits."

Her eyes widened. "What?"

"You heard me."

"I'm not property," she began.

"Neither am I, but don't start thinking about Cy, nevertheless. You can concentrate on me." He took one of her hands in his and looked at it, turning it over gently to study it. "Nice hands," he said. "Short nails, well-kept. No rings."

"I have several of them, mostly silver and turquoise, but I don't wear them very much."

His lean fingers rubbed gently over her ring finger and he looked thoughtful, absorbed.

Her own fingers went to the onyx-and-gold signet ring on the little finger of his left hand with the letter *S* in gold script embossed in the onyx.

"It was my father's," Eb told her solemnly. "He was a hell of a soldier, even if he wasn't the best father in the world."

"Do you miss him?" she asked gently.

He nodded. "I suppose I do, from time to time." He touched the ring. "This will go to my son, if I ever have one."

The thought of having children with Eb made Sally's knees weak, but she didn't speak. Eb seemed about to, when they were interrupted.

"Hey, Sally, look what I can do!" Stevie called, and executed a kick that sent the bag reeling.

"Very nice!" Eb said, grinning. "You're a quick study, young man."

"I got to learn to do it real fast," he murmured, sending another kick at the bag.

"Why?" Eb asked curiously.

"So I can hit that big blond man who makes my mama cry," he said, oblivious to the shocked and then amused looks on the faces of the adults near him.

"Dallas?" Sally asked.

"That's him," Stevie agreed, and his dark eyes glimmered. "Mama was crying last night and I asked her why, and she said that man hates her."

Eb joined the young boy at the bag and went on one knee beside him, his eyes very solemn. "Your mother and Dallas knew each other a long time ago," he told him in an adult way. "They had a fight, and they never made up. That's why she cried. They're both good people, Stevie, but sometimes even good people have arguments."

"Why are they mad at each other?"

"I don't know," Eb replied not quite factually. "That's for them to say, if they want you to know. Dallas isn't a bad man, though."

"He's all banged up," Stevie replied solemnly.

"Yes, he is. He was shot."

"Shot? Really?" Stevie moved closer to Eb and put a small hand on his shoulder. "Who shot him?"

"Some very bad men," Eb told him. "He almost died. That's why he has to use a walking stick now. It's why he has all those scars."

Stevie touched Eb's face. "You got scars, too."

"Yes, I have."

"You ever been shot?" he wanted to know.

"Several times," Eb replied honestly. "Guns can be very dangerous. I suppose you know that."

"I know it," Stevie said. "One of my friends shot himself with his dad's pistol playing war out in the yard. He was hurt pretty bad, but he's okay now. Mama told me that children should *never* touch a gun, even if they think it's not loaded."

"Good for your mom!"

"That man doesn't like my mama," he continued worriedly. "He frowns and frowns at her. She can't see it, but I see it."

"He wouldn't ever hurt her," Eb said firmly. "He's

there to protect her when you're away from home," he added wryly.

"That's right, I protect her at home. I'm very strong. See what I did to the bag?"

"I sure did!" Eb grinned at him. "Those were nice kicks, but you need to snap them out from the knee. Here—" he got to his feet "—let me show you."

Sally watched them with lazy pleasure, smiling at the born rapport between them. It was a pity that Stevie didn't like Dallas. That would matter one day. But she had enough problems of her own to worry about.

Eb stopped by the local sandwich shop and bought frozen yogurt cones for all three of them, a reward for the physical punishment, he told them dryly.

While the two adults sat at a table and ate their yogurt cones, Stevie became engrossed in some knickknacks on sale in the same store.

"He's a natural at this," Eb remarked.

"I'll bet I'm not," she mused, having had to repeat several of the moves quite a number of times before she did them well enough to suit her companion.

"You're not his age, either," he pointed out. "Most children learn things faster than adults. That's why they teach foreign languages so early these days."

"Do you speak any other languages?" she asked suddenly.

"Only a handful," he replied. "The romance languages, several dialects of African languages, and Russian."

"My goodness."

"Languages will get you far in intelligence work these days," he told her. "If you're going to work in foreign countries, it's stupid not to speak the language. It can get you killed."

"I had to have a foreign language series as part of my degree," she said. "I chose Spanish, because that's pretty necessary around here, with such a large Hispanic population. I hated it at first, and then I learned how to read in it." Her eyes brightened. "It's the most exciting thing in the world to read something in the language the author created it in. I never dreamed how delightful it would be to read *Don Quixote* as Cervantes actually wrote it!"

"I know what you mean. But the older the novel, the more difficult the translation. Words change meaning. And a good number of the more modern novels are written in the various dialects of Spanish provinces."

She grinned. "Like Blasco-Ibañez, who used a regional dialect for his matador hero, Juan Gallardo, in dialogue."

"Yes."

She finished her cone and wiped her hands. "I became really fascinated with bullfighting after I read the book, so I found a Web site that had biographies of all the matadors. I found the ones mentioned in the book, who fought in the corridas of Spain around the turn of the century."

"Until you read Blasco-Ibañez, you have no idea how dangerous bullfighting really is," Eb agreed. "He must have seen some of the corridas."

"A number of Spanish authors did. Lorca, for example, wrote a famous poem about the death of his friend Sanchez Mejias in the bullring."

He brushed back a strand of gold-streaked brown hair and smiled. "I've missed conversations like this, although a good many of the men I train are well-educated. In fact, Micah Steele, who does consulting work for me, was a resident doctor at one of the bigger Eastern hospitals when he joined my unit."

"Why did he give up a profession that he must have studied very hard for?"

"Nobody knows, and he won't talk. Mostly what we know about him we found out from his father, who used to be a bank president until his heart attack. Micah's stepsister, Callie, looks after old man Steele these days. He and Micah haven't spoken for years, not since he and Callie's mother divorced."

"Do you know why they did?"

He shrugged. "Local gossip had it that Micah's father caught Micah and his stepmother in a compromising position and threw them both out of the house."

"Poor man."

"Poor Callie. She worshiped the ground Micah walked on, but he won't even speak to her these days."

"That name sounds familiar," she commented.

"It should. Callie's a paralegal. She works for Barnes and Kemp, the trial lawyers here in town."

"It's so nice to have a lazy day like this," she murmured, watching Stevie browse among the party decorations on a shelf. "It makes me forget the danger."

"I'm surprised that Lopez hasn't made any more moves lately," he said. "And a little disturbed. It isn't like him to back off."

"Maybe he was afraid those two men who attacked me would be arrested and they'd tell on him," she said.

He laughed mirthlessly. "Dream on. Lopez would have them disposed of before they had time to rat on him." He pursed his lips. "That could be what happened to them. You don't make a mistake when you belong to that particular cartel. No second chances. Ever."

She shivered. "We do keep all the doors locked," she said. "And we're very careful about what we say. Well, Jessica is," she amended sheepishly. "Until you taught me about surveillance equipment, I didn't know that a whisper could be heard half a mile away."

"Never forget it," he told her. "Never drop your guard, either. I'll always have someone close enough to run interference if you get into trouble, but you have to do your part to keep the house secure."

"And let you know when and where I'm going," she agreed. "I won't forget again."

He reached across the table and folded his fingers into hers, liking the way they clung. His thumb smoothed over the soft, moist palm while he searched her eyes.

"You haven't had an easy time of it, have you?" he asked conversationally. "In some ways, your whole life has been in turmoil since you were seventeen."

"In transition, at least," she corrected, smiling gently. "If there's one thing I've learned, it's that everything changes."

"I suppose so." His fingers tightened on hers and the look in his eyes was suddenly dark and mysterious and a little threatening. "I've learned a few things myself," he said quietly.

"Such as?" she whispered daringly.

He glanced down at their entwined fingers. "Such as never taking things for granted."

She frowned, puzzled.

He laughed and let go of her fingers. "I told you that I was engaged once, didn't I?" he asked.

She nodded.

"I never told her what I did for a living. She never questioned where my money came from. In fact, when I tried to tell her, she stopped me, saying it wouldn't matter, that she loved me and she'd go wherever my job took me." He leaned back in his chair, his expression reflective and solemn. "Her parents were dead. She and an older boy were fostered at the same time to a wealthy woman.

They spent years together, but he and Maggie weren't close, so I made all the wedding arrangements and paid for her gown and the rings, everything.'' His eyes darkened with remembered pain. ''I still felt uncomfortable about having secrets between us, though, so the night before the wedding, I told her what I did for a living. She put the rings on the coffee table, got her stuff, and left town that same night. She married two months later...a man twice her age.''

She knew about his ex-fiancée, but not how much he'd cared about the woman. The expression in his eyes told her that the pain hadn't gone away. ''Didn't she send you a letter, or phone you after she'd had time to think it over?'' she asked.

He shook his head. ''Until I ran into her in Houston a week ago, I had no idea where she was. Her adoptive mother died just after we broke up. Tough break.''

Her heart stopped in her chest. ''You...saw her...in Houston?''

He nodded, oblivious to the shock in her eyes. ''As luck would have it, she's a new junior partner in an investment firm I use, and widowed.''

He stared at her until she looked up, and he wasn't smiling. ''You're in a precarious situation, and we've been thrown together in a rather unconventional way. We're friends, but you don't have to live with what I do.''

All her hopes and dreams and wild expectations crumbled to dust in her mind. Friends. Good friends. Of course they were! He was teaching her martial arts, he was helping her to survive a potential attack by a ruthless drug lord. That didn't mean he wanted her to share his life. Quite the opposite, it seemed now.

"If a woman cared enough, surely she could give it a chance?" she asked, terrified that her anguish might show.

Apparently it didn't. He leaned back in his chair with a long sigh, reflective and moody. "No. She said she wanted a career, anyway," he replied. "It suited her to have her own money and be independent."

"My parents never shared their paychecks, or anything else," she said carelessly. She finished her cone and glanced at Stevie. "Stevie, we'd better go, sweetheart."

He came running, smiling as he leaned against her and looked across at Eb, who was still brooding. "Can we take Mama a cone?"

"Of course we can," Sally said gently. She dug out two dollars. "Here. Get her a cup of that fat-free Dutch chocolate, okay? And make sure it has a lid."

"Okay!"

He ran off with his grubstake, feeling very adult. Sally watched him, smiling.

"I could have done that," Eb commented.

"Yes, you could, but it wouldn't help teach him responsibility. Six isn't too young to start learning independence. He's going to be a fine man," she added, her voice softer as she watched him.

He didn't comment. He was feeling claustrophobic and he didn't know why. He got up and dealt with the used napkins. By the time he was finished, Stevie came back carrying a small white sack with Jessica's treat inside.

There wasn't much conversation on the way back to the Johnson house, and even then it was completely impersonal. Sally realized that it must have hurt Eb to recall how abruptly his fiancée had rejected him. She might have loved him, but the constant danger of his profession must have been more than she could handle. Now that he was retired from the danger, it might not be such an obstacle.

That was a depressing thought. His ex-fiancée was a widow and he was in a secure profession, and they'd recently seen each other. It was enough to get Sally out of the truck with Stevie and off into the house with only a quick thank-you and a forced smile.

Eb, driving away down the road, felt a vague regret for the loss of the rapport he and Sally had seemed to share. He couldn't understand what had made her so distant this afternoon.

Eb had already contacted a man he knew in the Drug Enforcement Administration on a secure channel and told him what he knew about Lopez and his plans for Jacobsville. He'd also asked about the possibility of having a man go undercover to infiltrate the operation and was told only that the DEA was aware of Lopez's construction project. He wouldn't tell Eb anything more than that.

Understanding government work very well, Eb had assumed that the undercover operation was already underway. He wasn't about to mention that to anyone he knew. Not even Cy.

He had Dallas monitoring some sensitive equipment that gave them direct audio and visual information from Sally's house. Nobody would sneak up on it without being noticed. He'd also had Dallas bug the telephone. That night, he was glad he had.

In the early hours of the morning, Sally was brought wide-awake by the insistent ringing of the telephone. The number was unlisted, but that didn't stop telemarketers. Ordinarily, though, they didn't call at this hour. It wasn't a good marketing strategy, especially in Sally's case. She'd hardly slept after the discussion with Eb in the yogurt shop. She wasn't in the mood to talk to strangers.

"Hello?" she asked belligerently.

"You'll never see us coming," a slow, ice-cold voice said in her ear. "But unless Jessica gives up the name by midnight Saturday, there will be serious repercussions."

Sally was so shocked that she fumbled with the phone and cut off the caller. She stood holding the receiver, blinking in astonishment. That softly accented tone had chilled her to the bone, despite the flannel gown she was wearing.

No sooner had she righted the telephone than it rang again. This time, she hesitated. Her heart was pounding like mad. She was almost shaking with the force of it. Her mouth was dry. Her palms began to sweat. There was an uncomfortable knot in the pit of her stomach.

She wanted to ignore it. She didn't dare. Quickly, before she lost her nerve, she lifted it.

"She has one last chance," the voice continued, as if the connection hadn't been cut. "She must phone this number Saturday night at midnight exactly and give a name. One minute after midnight, you will all suffer the consequences." He gave the number and hung up. This time the connection was cut even more rapidly. Sally dropped the receiver back into the cradle with icy fingers. She stared down at it with growing horror. Surely Eb and Dallas and the others would be watching. But were they listening as well?

The phone rang a third time, but now she was angry and she didn't hesitate. She jerked it up. "Hello...?"

"We couldn't get a trace," Eb said angrily. "Are you all right?"

She swallowed, closed her eyes, took a deep breath, and

swallowed again. "Yes," she said calmly. "I'm all right. You heard what he said?"

"I heard. Don't worry."

"Don't worry?" she parroted. "When a man's just threatened to kill everyone in my house?"

"He won't kill anybody," he assured her. "And he's through making threats for tonight. I'm going to find out where that phone is. Go to sleep. It's all right."

The receiver went dead. "I am sick and tired of men throwing out orders and hanging up on me!" she told the telephone earpiece.

It did no good, of course, except that voicing her irritation made her feel a little better. She climbed back into bed and lay awake, wide-eyed and nervous, until dawn. Just before she and Stevie left for school, out of the child's hearing range, she told Jessica what had happened.

"Eb and the others are watching us," Sally assured her quickly. "But be careful about answering the door."

"No need," Jessica said. "Lopez may be certifiable, but he's predictable. He never takes action until his demands haven't been met. We have until midnight Saturday to think of something."

"Wonderful," Sally said on a sigh. "We have today and tomorrow. I'm sure we'll have Lopez and all his cohorts in jail by then."

"Sarcasm doesn't suit you, dear," Jessica said with a smile. "Go to work. I'll be fine."

"I wish I could guarantee that all of us would be fine," Sally murmured to herself as she went out the door behind Stevie.

Somehow she knew that life would never be the same again. It had been bad enough hearing Eb talk about the woman he'd loved who had rejected him at the altar, and knowing from the way he spoke of it that he hadn't gotten over her. But now, she had drug dealers threatening to kill Jessica and Stevie as well as herself. She wondered how in the world she'd ended up in such a nightmare.

It didn't help when Eb phoned again and told her that the phone number she'd been given was that of a stolen cell phone, untraceable until it was answered, and it rang and rang unnoticed now. There would be no time to run a trace precisely at midnight. It was the most disheartening news Sally had received in a long time.

Chapter Seven

Eb was disturbed by the message he'd intercepted from Lopez. He knew, even better than Sally did, that it wasn't an idle threat. The drug lord, like his minions, was merciless. He'd had countless enemies neutralized, and he wouldn't hesitate because Jessica was a woman. Just the month before his arrest, he'd had the leader of a drug-dealing gang disposed of for cheating him. It was chilling even for a professional soldier to know what depths a human being could sink to in the name of greed.

He and Dallas started planning for the certainty of an attack. The Johnson homeplace was isolated, but it had plenty of cover where men could hide. Eb intended having people in place long before Lopez's hired goons could find a safe passage to the house to carry out the madman's orders. Anything else would be impossible, since he knew Jessica would never sacrifice her informant's life, even to save herself and her family.

''I think we can safely assume that these men aren't

professionals," Dallas said quietly. "Their way will be to wade in shooting."

Eb's pale eyes narrowed. "I wouldn't bet the lives of two women and a child on that," he replied. "Lopez knows I'm here, and that I have trained professionals working for me. He also knows that I'm why Jessica talked Sally into moving back here in the first place. He's ruthless, but he isn't stupid. When he comes after Jessica, he'll send the best people he's got."

"Point taken," Dallas said heavily. "I suppose it was wishful thinking." He glanced worriedly at Eb. "We could bring all three of them over here."

"Sure we could. But it would only postpone the inevitable. Lopez doesn't quit. He'll look on it as a setback and find another way to get to them. Besides, they can't stay here indefinitely. Sally has a job and Stevie has to go to school."

Dallas stared into the distance, quiet and thoughtful. "Stevie doesn't like me," he murmured. "He told his mother he was learning karate so that he could work me over." He shot a half-amused glance in Eb's direction. "Spunky kid."

"Yes, he is," Eb agreed. "Pity he has to grow up without a father. And before you fly at me," he interrupted Dallas's exclamation, "I know Jessica didn't tell you whose child he was. But you know now."

"I know," Dallas muttered irritably, "for all the good it does me. She won't even discuss it. The minute I walk in the door, she clams up and stays that way until I leave. I can barely get her to say hello and goodbye!"

"Then she cries herself to sleep at night because you hate her."

The blond man's dark eyes widened. *"What?"*

"That's why Stevie wants to deck you," Eb said simply. "He's very protective of his mother."

Dallas seemed to calm down a little. "Imagine that," he mused. "Well, well. So she isn't quite as disinterested as she pretends." He stuck his hands into his pockets and leaned back against the wall. "No chance she'll turn in the guy who ratted on Lopez, I gather?"

"Not one in a million." He studied the other man for a moment. "You're really worried."

"Of course I am. I've seen the aftermath of Lopez's vendettas," Dallas said curtly. "What worries me most is that if someone's willing to trade his life or his freedom to get you, he can. No protection is adequate against a determined killer."

"Then ours will make history," Eb promised him. "Let's go over to Cy Parks's place. I want to see if he's got a way to contact that guy in Mexico who used to work as a mercenary with Dutch Van Meer and Diego Laremos back in the eighties. He went on to do work infiltrating drug cartels."

"J.D. Brettman led that mercenary group," Dallas recalled, grinning. "He's a superior court judge in Chicago these days. Imagine that!"

"I heard that Van Meer lives with his wife and kids in the northwestern Rocky Mountains on a ranch. What about Laremos?" Eb asked.

"He and his family live in the Yucatán. He's given up soldiering, too." He shook his head. "Those guys were younger than us when they started and they made fortunes."

"It was a different game back then. Times have changed. So have the rules. We'd never get away with some of the stunts those guys pulled." Eb felt in his pocket for his truck keys. "All of us met them, but Cy and Diego

Laremos got to know each other well several years back when Cy was doing a little job down around Cancún for a wealthy yachtsman. He may know the professional soldier who helped a friend of Laremos's escape some nasty pothunters and a kidnapper.''

"Do I know this friend?'' Dallas wanted to know as they headed out the door.

"You probably know *of* him—Canton Rourke.''

"Good Lord, Mr. Software?'' Dallas exclaimed. "The guy who lost everything and then regrouped and now has a corporation in the Fortune 500?''

"That's him.'' Eb nodded. "Turns out the new Mrs. Rourke's parents are university professors who devote summers to Mayan digs in the Yucatán. It's a long story, but this Mexican agent does a little freelance work. He'd be an asset in this sort of operation.''

"He might even have some contacts we could use?''

"That's so.'' Eb got in and started the truck. He glanced at Dallas. "Besides that, he's done undercover work on narcotics smuggling for the Mexican government and lived to tell about it. That proves how good he is. A lot of undercover people get killed.''

"He'd be just what we need, if we can get him. I don't imagine the DEA is going to tell us who their undercover guy is, or what he finds out.''

"Exactly. That's where I hope Cy's going to come in. He doesn't like any of the old associations very much anymore, but considering the danger Lopez poses, he might be willing to help us.''

"Pity about his arm.''

Eb shot him a wry glance. "Yes, but it's a lucky break it wasn't the arm he uses.''

They drove over to Cy Parks's ranch, and found him watching his young foreman, Harley, doctoring a sick bull yearling in the barn. He was lounging against one of the posts that supported the imposing structure, his hat low over his eyes, his arms folded over a broad chest, one booted foot resting on a rail of the gate that enclosed the stall where his man was busy.

He turned as Cy and Dallas strode down the neat chipped bark covered floor to join him.

"You two out sightseeing?" Cy drawled without smiling, his green eyes narrowed and curious.

"Not today. We need a name."

"Whose?"

"The guy who worked with your friend Diego Laremos out near Chichén Itzá. I think he might be just what we need to infiltrate Lopez's cartel."

Cy's eyebrows lifted. "Rodrigo? You must be out of your mind!" he said at once.

"Why?"

"Good God," Cy burst out, "Diego says that he's such a renegade, nobody will hire him anymore, not even for black ops!"

"What did he do?" Dallas asked, aware that the young man in the stall had perked up and was suddenly listening unashamedly.

"For a start, he crashed a Huey out in the Yucatán last year," Cy said. "That didn't endear him to a certain government agency which was running him. Then he blew up an entire boatload of powder cocaine off Cozumel that the authorities were trying to confiscate—millions' worth. In between he wrecked a few hired cars in various chases, hijacked a plane, and broke into a government field office. He walked off with a couple of classified files and several thousand dollars' worth of high-tech listening devices that you can't even buy unless you're in law enforcement. After that, he went berserk in a bar down in Panama and put two men in the hospital, just before he absconded with a suitcase full of unlaundered drug money that belonged to Manuel Lopez…''

"Are we talking about the same Rodrigo that the feds used to call 'Mr. Cool'?" Eb asked with evident surprise.

"That isn't what they call him these days," Cy said flatly. "Mr. Liability would be more like it."

"He was with Laremos and Van Meer in Africa back in the early eighties," Eb recalled. "They left, but he signed on with another outfit and kept going."

"That's when he started working freelance for the feds," Cy continued. "At least, that's what Diego said," he added for Harley's benefit. He didn't want his young employee to know about his past.

"Anybody know why Rodrigo went bananas in Panama?" Dallas asked.

Cy shrugged. "There are a lot of rumors—but nothing concrete." He studied the other two with pursed lips. "If you want him for undercover work to indict Lopez, he'd probably pay you to hire him on. He hates Lopez."

Eb glanced past Cy at Harley, whose mouth was hanging open.

"Don't mind him," Cy told his companions with a mocking smile. "He's a mercenary, too," he added dryly.

Harley scrambled to his feet. "Can't I hire on?" he burst out. "Listen, I know those names—Van Meer and Brettman and Laremos. They were legends!"

"Put the top back on the medicine before you spill it," Cy told the young man calmly. "As for the other, that's up to Eb. It's his party."

Harley fumbled the lid back on the bottle. "Mr. Scott?" he asked, pleading.

"I guess we could find you something to do," Eb said, amused. Then the smile faded, and his whole look was threatening. "But this is strictly on the QT. You breathe one word of it locally and you're out on your ear. Got that?"

Harley nodded eagerly. "Sure!"

"And you'll work for him only after you do your chores here," Cy said firmly. "I run cattle, not commandos."

"Yes, sir!"

Cy exchanged a complicated glance with Eb. "I've got the last number I had for Rodrigo in my office. I'll go get it."

He left the other three men in the barn. Harley was almost dancing with excitement.

"I'll be an asset, sir, honestly," he told Eb. "I can shoot anything that has bullets, and use a knife, and I know a little martial arts…!"

Eb chuckled. "Son, we don't need an assassin. We're collecting intelligence."

The boy's face fell. "Oh."

"Running gun battles aren't a big part of the business," Dallas said without cracking a smile. "You shoot anybody these days, even a criminal, and you could find yourself behind bars."

Harley looked shocked. "But…but I read about it all the time; those exciting battles in Africa…"

"Exciting?" Eb's eyes were steady and quiet.

"Why, sure!" Harley's eyes lit up. "You know, testing your courage under fire."

The boy's eyes were gleaming with excitement, and Eb knew then for certain that he'd never seen anyone shot. Probably the closest he'd come to it was listening to an instructor—probably a retired mercenary—talking about combat.

Harley noticed his employer coming out of the house and he grimaced. "I hope Mr. Parks meant what he said.

He's not much on adventure, you see. He's sort of sarcastic when I mention where I went on my vacation, out in the field in Central America with a group of mercenaries. It was great!''

"Cy wasn't enthusiastic, I gather?" Eb probed.

"Naw," Harley said heavily. "He's just a rancher. Even if he knows Mr. Laremos, he sure doesn't know what it's like to really be a soldier of fortune. But we do, don't we?" he asked the other two with a grin.

Eb and Dallas glanced at each other and managed not to laugh. Quite obviously, Harley believed that Cy's information about Rodrigo was secondhand and had no idea what Cy did before he became a rancher.

Cy joined them, presenting a slip of paper with a number on it to Eb. "That's the last number I have, but they'll relay it, I'm sure."

"You still hear from Laremos?" Eb asked his friend.

"Every year, at Christmas," Cy told him. "They've got three kids now and the eldest is in high school." He shook his head. "I'm getting old."

"Not you," Eb chuckled.

"We'd better go," Dallas said, checking his watch.

"So we had."

"What about me?" Harley asked excitedly.

"We'll be in touch, when the time comes," Eb promised him, and, oddly, it sounded more like a threat.

Cy saw them off and came back to take one last look at the bull. "Good job, Harley," he said, approving the treatment. "You'll make a rancher yet."

Harley closed the bull in his stall and latched the gate. "How do you know Mr. Laremos, sir?" he asked curiously.

"Oh, we had a mutual acquaintance," he said without meeting the other man's eyes. "Diego still keeps in touch with the old group, so he knows what's going on in the intelligence field," he added deliberately.

"I see. I thought it was probably something like that," Harley said absently and went to work on the calf with scours in the next stall, reaching for the pills that were commonly called "eggs" to dose it with.

Cy looked after the smug younger man with amusement. Harley had his boss pegged as a retiring, staid rancher with no backbone and only an outsider's familiarity with the world of covert operations. He'd think that Cy had gotten all that information from Laremos, and, for the present, it suited Cy very well to let him think so. But if Harley had in mind an adventure with Eb and the others, he was in for a real shock. In the company of those men, he was going to be more uncomfortable than he dreamed right now. Some lessons, he told himself, were better learned through experience.

When they got back to the ranch, Eb phoned the number Cy had given him. There was a long pause and then a quick, deep voice giving instructions. Eb was to leave his name and number and hang up immediately. He did. Seconds later, his phone rang.

"You run that strategy and tactics school in Texas," the deep voice said evenly.

"Yes."

"I read about it in one of the intelligence sitreps," he returned, shortening the name for situation reports. "I thought you were one of those vacation mercs who sat at a desk all week and liked to play at war a couple of weeks a year, until I spoke to Laremos. He remembers you, along with another Jacobsville resident named Parks."

"Cy and I used to work together, with Dallas Kirk and Micah Steele," Eb replied quietly.

"I don't know them, but I know Parks. If you're looking for someone to do black ops, I'm not available," he said curtly, with only a trace of an accent. "I don't do overseas work anymore, either. There's a fairly large price on my head in certain Latin American circles."

"It isn't a foreign job. I want someone to go undercover here in Texas and relay intelligence from a drug cartel," Eb said flatly.

There was a long pause. "I'd find someone with a terminal illness for that sort of work," Rodrigo replied. "It's usually fatal."

"Cy Parks told me you'd probably jump at the chance to do this job."

"Oh, that's rich. And what job would that be?"

"The drug lord I want intelligence on is Manuel Lopez. I'm trying to put him back in prison permanently."

The intake of breath on the other end was audible, followed by a description of Lopez that questioned his ancestry, his paternity, his morals, and various other facets of his life in both Spanish and English.

"That's the very Lopez I'm talking about," Eb replied dryly. "Interested?"

"In killing him, yes. Putting him back in prison...well, he can still run the cartel from there."

"While he's in there, his organization could be successfully infiltrated and destroyed from within," Eb suggested, dangling the idea like a carrot on a string. "In fact, the reason we're under the gun in Jacobsville right now is because a friend of our group is protecting the identity of an intimate of Lopez who sold him out to the DEA."

"Keep talking," Rodrigo said at once.

"Lopez is trying to kill a former government agent who coaxed one of his intimate friends to help her get the hard evidence to put him in prison. He's only out on a legal

technicality and he's apparently using his temporary freedom to dispose of her and her informant.''

"What about the so-called hard evidence?" Rodrigo
asked.

"My guess is that it'll disappear before the retrial. If he
manages to get rid of the witnesses and destroy the evidence, he'll never go back to prison. In fact, he's already
skipped bond.''

"Don't tell me. They set bail at a million dollars and
he paid it out of petty cash," came the sarcastic reply.

"Exactly.''

There was a brief hesitation and a sigh. "Well, in that
case, I suppose I'm working for you.''

Eb smiled. "I'll put you on the payroll.''

"Fine, but you can forget about retirement benefits if I
go undercover.''

Eb chuckled softly. "There's just one thing. We've
heard that you and Lopez had a common interest at one
time," he said, putting it as delicately as he could. "Does
he know what you look like?"

There was another pause and when the voice came back,
it was strained. "No, you can be sure of that.''

"This won't be easy," Eb told him. "Be sure you're
willing to take the risk before you agree.''

"I'm quite sure. I'll see you tomorrow." The line went
dead.

Eb took Sally out to dinner that night, driving the sleek
new black Jaguar S that he liked to use when he went to
town.

"We'll go to Houston, if that suits you?"

She agreed. He looked devastating in a dinner jacket,
and she was shy and uneasy with him, after what she'd
learned about his fiancée. In fact, she'd told herself she

wasn't going to be alone with him ever again. Yet here she sat. Resolve was hard when emotions were involved. His feelings for the woman he'd planned to marry were unmistakable in his voice when he talked about her, and now that she was free, he might have a second chance. Knowing that part of him had never gotten over his fiancée's defection, Sally was reluctant to risk her heart on him again. She kept a smiling, pleasant, but determined distance between them.

Eb noticed the reticence, but didn't understand its purpose. He could hardly take his eyes off her tonight. His green eyes kept returning to linger on her pretty black cocktail dress under the long red-lined black velvet coat she wore with it. Her hair was in a neat chignon at her nape, and she looked lovely.

"Are you sure this is a good idea?" Sally asked him. "I know Dallas will take care of Jess and Stevie, but it seems risky to go out at night with Lopez and his men around."

"He's a vicious devil," he replied, "but he is absolutely predictable. He'll give Jessica until exactly midnight Saturday. He won't do one thing until the deadline. At one minute past midnight," he added curtly, "there will be an assault."

Sally wrapped her arms closer around her body. "How do we end up with people like that in the world?"

"We forget that all lives are interconnected in some way, and that selfishness and greed are not desirable traits."

"What good will it do Lopez to kill Jessica and us?" she asked curiously. "I know he's angry at her, but if she's dead, she can't tell him anything!"

"He's going to be setting an example," he said. "Of

course, he probably thinks she'll give up the name to save her child." He glanced at Sally. "Would you?"

"I wouldn't have a hard time choosing between my child and someone who's already turned against his own people," she admitted.

"Jessica says there are extenuating circumstances," he told her.

She stared at her fingers. "I know. She won't even tell me who the person was." She glanced at him. "She's probably covering all her bases. If I knew who it was..."

He made a sound deep in his throat. "You'd turn the person over to Lopez?"

She shifted restlessly. "I might."

"Cows might fly."

He knew her too well. She laughed softly. "I wish there was another way out of this, that's all. I don't want Stevie hurt."

"He won't be." He reached across to clasp her cool hand gently in hers and press it. "I'm putting together a network. Lopez isn't going to be able to move without being in someone's line of sight from now on."

"I wish..." she began.

"Don't wish your life away. You have to take the bad with the good—that's what life is. Good times don't make us strong."

She grimaced. "No. I guess they don't." She leaned her head back against the headrest and drank in the smell of the leather. "I love the way new cars smell," she said conversationally. "And this one is just super."

"It has a few minor modifications," he said absently.

She turned her head toward him with a wicked grin. "Don't tell me—the headlights retract and become machine gun ports, the tailpipe leaves oil slicks, and the passenger seat is really an ejectable projectile!"

He laughed. "Not quite."

"Spoilsport."

"You need to stop watching old James Bond movies," he pointed out. "The world has changed since the sixties."

Her eyes studied his profile quietly. He was still handsome well into his thirties, and he glorified evening clothes. She knew that she couldn't look forward to anything permanent with him, but sometimes just looking at him was almost enough. He was devastating.

He caught that scrutiny and glanced at her, enjoying the shy admiration in her gray eyes. "Can you dance?" he asked.

"I'm not in the class with Matt Caldwell on a dance floor," she teased, "but I can hold my own, I suppose. Are we going dancing?"

"We're going to a supper club where they have an orchestra and a dance floor," he said. "A sophisticated place with a few carefully placed friends of mine."

"I should have known."

"You'll like it," he promised. "You'll never spot them. They blend in."

"You don't blend," she murmured dryly.

He chuckled. "If that's a compliment, thank you," he said.

"It was."

"You won't blend, either," he said in a low, soft tone.

She clutched her small bag tightly in her lap, feeling the softness right through her body. It made her giddy to think of being held in his arms on a dance floor. It was something she'd dreamed about in her senior year of high school, but it had never happened. As if it would have. She couldn't really picture Eb at a high school prom.

"You're sure Jess and Stevie will be okay?" she asked

as he pulled off the main highway and onto a Houston city street.

"I'm sure. Dallas is inside and I have a few people outside. But I meant what I said," he added solemnly. "Lopez won't do a thing until midnight tomorrow."

She supposed that was a sort of knowledge of the enemy that came from long experience in a dangerous profession. But she couldn't help worrying about her family. If anything happened while she was away, she'd never forgive herself.

The club was just off a main thoroughfare, and so discreet that it wouldn't have drawn attention to itself. The luxury cars in the parking lot were an intimation of what was inside.

Inside, the sounds of music came from a room off the main hallway. There was a bar and a small coffee shop, apart from the restaurant. Inside, an employee in a dinner jacket led them into the restaurant, which ringed a central dance floor, where a small jazz ensemble played lazy blues tunes for several couples who were dancing.

"This is really spectacular," she told Eb when they were seated near a small indoor waterfall with tropical plants blooming around it.

"It is, isn't it?" he asked, leaning back to study her with a warm smile. "I have to admit, it's one of my favorite haunts when I'm in Houston."

"I can see why." She searched his eyes in a long, tense silence.

He didn't smile. His eyes narrowed as they locked into hers. She could almost hear her own heart beating, beating, beating…!

"Why, Eb!" came a soft voice from behind Sally.

"What a coincidence to find you here, at one of our favorite night spots."

Without another word being spoken, Sally knew the identity of the newcomer. It couldn't be anyone except Eb's ex-fiancée.

Chapter Eight

"Hello, Maggie," Eb said, standing up to greet the pretty green-eyed brunette who took possession of his arm and smiled up at him.

"It's good to see you again so soon!" she said with obvious pleasure. "You remember Cord Romero, don't you?" She indicated a tall, dark-haired, dark-eyed man beside her without meeting his eyes. "He and I were fostered together by Mrs. Amy Barton, the Houston socialite."

"Sure. How are you, Cord?" Eb asked.

The other man, his equal in height and build, nodded. Sally was curious about Maggie's obvious uneasiness around the other man.

"Sally, this is Maggie Barton and Cord Romero. Sally Johnson." They all acknowledged the introductions, and Eb added, "Won't you join us?"

Sally's heart plummeted as she saw Maggie's eyes light up at the invitation and knew she wouldn't refuse.

"We may be intruding," Cord said with a pointed look at Sally.

"Oh, not at all," Sally said at once.

"I thought Sally needed a night out," Eb said easily and with a warm smile in Sally's direction. "She's an elementary schoolteacher."

The man, Cord, studied her with open curiosity while Eb seated Maggie.

"Allow me," Cord said smoothly, standing behind Sally's chair.

Sally smiled at the old-world courtesy. "Thank you."

Eb glanced at them with unreadable eyes before he turned back to Maggie, who was flushed and avoided looking at the other couple. "Quite a coincidence, running into you here," he said in a neutral tone.

"It was Cord's idea," Maggie said. "He felt like a night on the town and he doesn't date these days. Better your foster sister than nobody, right, Cord?" she added with a nervous laugh and a smile that didn't touch her eyes.

Cord shrugged broad shoulders indolently and didn't say a word, but his distaste for her reference was there, in those unblinking dark eyes.

Sally was curious about him. She wondered what he did for a living. He was very fit for a man his age, which she judged to be about the same as Eb's. His hands were rough and callused, as if he worked physically rather than sat behind a desk. He had the same odd stare that she'd noticed in Eb and Dallas and even Cy Parks, a probing but unfocused distant stare that held a strange hollowness.

"How are things going at the ranch?" Maggie asked gently. "I heard that you had Dallas out there with you."

"Yes," he replied. "He's doing some consulting work for me."

"Shot to pieces, wasn't he?" Cord asked abruptly, his eyes on Sally's face.

"That happens when a man doesn't keep his mind on

his work," Eb said with a pointed glance at Cord, who averted his eyes.

"One of my friends is hosting a huge party down in Cancún for Christmas," Maggie murmured, drawing a lazy polished nail across the back of Eb's hand. "Why don't you take some time off and go with me?"

"No time," Eb said with a smile to soften the words. "I'm not a man of leisure."

"Baloney," she replied. "You could retire on what you've got squirreled away."

"And do what?" came the dry response. "Do I look like a lounge lizard to you?"

"I didn't mean that," she said, and her eyes searched his face for a long moment. "I meant that you could give up walking into danger if you wanted to."

"That's an old argument and you know what the answer is," Eb told her bluntly.

She withdrew her hand from his with a sad little sigh. "Yes, I know," she said wearily. "It's in your blood and you can't stop." Involuntarily she glanced at Cord.

Eb frowned a little as he watched her wilt. Sally saw it and knew at once that he and Maggie had gone through that very argument years ago when she'd broken their engagement. It wasn't their emotions that had split them up. It was his job that he wouldn't quit, not even for a woman he'd loved enough to marry.

She felt helpless. She'd known at some level that he was carrying a torch for Maggie. She stared at her own short, unpolished nails and compared them with Maggie's long, red-stained, beautiful ones. The difference was like the women themselves—one colorful and flamboyant and drawing attention, the other reclusive and practical and...dull. No wonder Eb hadn't wanted her all those years ago. Beside the exotic Maggie, she was insignificant.

"What subject is your specialty, Miss Johnson?" Cord asked curiously.

"History, actually," she said. "But I teach second grade, so I'm not really using it."

"No ambition to teach higher grades?" he persisted.

She shook her head and smiled wryly. "I tried it when I did my practice-teaching," she confessed. "And by the end of the day, my classroom was more like a zoo than a regimented place of learning. I'm afraid I don't have the facility to handle discipline at a higher level."

Cord's lean face lightened just a little as he studied her. "I had the facility, but the principal and the school board didn't like my methods," he replied.

"You teach?" she asked, enthused to find a colleague in such an unlikely place.

"I taught high school science for a year after I got out of college," he said. "But it wasn't a profession I could love enough to continue." He shrugged. "I found I had an aptitude in a totally unrelated area."

Maggie's hand clenched on her water glass and she took a quick sip.

"What do you do?" she asked, fascinated.

He glanced at Eb, who was openly glaring at him. "Ask Eb," he said on a brief, deep laugh, with a cold glance in Maggie's direction. "Can we order now?" he asked, lifting the menu. "I haven't even had lunch today."

Eb signaled a waiter and brought Sally's conversation with Cord to an end.

It was the longest and most tense meal Sally could remember having sat through. Maggie and Eb talked about places and people that they shared in memory while Sally concentrated on her food.

Cord was polite, but he made no further attempt at conversation. At the end of the evening, as the two couples parted outside the restaurant, Maggie held on to Eb's hand until he had to forcibly draw it away from her.

"Can't you come up and have dinner with us again one evening?" Maggie asked plaintively.

"Perhaps," Eb said with a careless smile. He glanced at Cord. "Good to see you."

Cord nodded. He glanced down at Sally. "Nice to have met you, Miss Johnson."

"Same here," she said with a smile.

Maggie hesitated and looked uneasy as Eb deliberately took her arm and propelled her away. She went with him, but her back was arrow-straight and she looked as if she was walking on hot coals and on the way to her own execution.

Eb stared after them for a long moment before he put Sally into the sleek Jaguar and climbed in under the wheel. He gave her a look that could have curdled milk.

"Don't encourage him," he said at once.

Her mouth fell open. "W…what?"

"You heard me." He started the car, and turned toward Sally. His eyes went over her like sensual fingers, brushing her throat, her bare shoulders under the coat, the shadowy hollow in her breasts revealed by the low-cut dress. "He has a weakness for blondes. He was ravishing you with his eyes."

She didn't know how to respond. While Sally was trying to come up with a response, he moved closer and slid a hand under her nape, under the heavy coil of hair, and pulled her face up toward his.

"So was I," he whispered roughly, and his mouth went down on her lips, burrowing beneath them, pressing them apart, devouring them. At the same time, his free hand slid right down into the low bodice of her dress and curved around her warm, bare breast.

"Eb!" she choked, stiffening.

He was undeterred. He groaned, overcome with desire, and his fingers contracted in a slow, heated, sensual rhythm that brought Sally's mouth open in a tiny gasp. His tongue found the unprotected heat of it and moved inside, in lazy, teasing motions that made her whole body clench.

He felt her nervous fingers fumble against the front of his dress shirt. Impatiently, he unfastened three buttons and dragged her hand inside the shirt, over hair-roughened muscles down to a nipple as hard as the one pressing feverishly into the palm of his hand.

She was devastated by the passion that had kindled so unexpectedly. She couldn't find the strength or the voice to protest the liberties he was taking, or to care that they were in a public parking lot. She didn't care about anything except making sure that he didn't stop. He couldn't stop. He mustn't stop, he mustn't...!

But he did, suddenly. He held her hands together tightly as he moved a little away from her, painfully aware that she was trying to get back into his arms.

"No," he said curtly, and shook her clenched hands.

She stared into his blazing eyes, her breath rustling in her throat, her heartbeat visible at the twin points so blatantly obvious against the bodice of her dress.

He glanced down at her and his jaw clenched. His own body was in agony, and this would only get worse if he didn't stop them now. She was too responsive, too tempting. He was going to have to make sure that he didn't touch her that way when they were completely alone. The consequences could be devastating. It was the wrong time for a torrid relationship. If he let himself lose his head over Sally right now, it could cost all of them their lives.

Forcefully, he put her back into her own seat and fastened the seat belt around her.

She just stared at him with those huge, soulful gray eyes that made him feel hungry and guilt-ridden all at the same time.

"I have to get you home," he said tersely.

She nodded. Her throat was too tight for words to get out. She clutched her small purse in her hands and stared out the window as he put the car into gear and pulled out into traffic.

It was a long, and very silent, drive back to her house. He was preoccupied, as distant as she remembered him from her teens. She wondered if he was thinking about Maggie and regretting the decision he'd made that put her out of his life. She was mature now, but beautiful as well, and it didn't take a mind reader to know that she was still attracted to Eb. How he felt was less obvious. He was a man who knew how to hide what he felt, and that skill was working overtime tonight.

"Why did Maggie introduce Cord as a foster child at first and then refer to him as her brother? Are they related?" she asked.

"They are not," he returned flatly. "His parents died in a fire, and she came from a severely disfunctional family. Mrs. Barton adopted both of them. Maggie took her name, but Cord kept his own. His father was a rather famous matador in Spain until his death. Maggie does usually try to present Cord as her brother. She's scared to death of him, despite the fact that they've kept in close touch all these years."

That was a surprise. "But why is she scared of him?"

He chuckled. "Because she wants him, although she's apparently never realized it," he returned with a quick glance. "He's been a colleague of mine for a long time, and I always thought that Maggie got engaged to me to put Cord out of the reach of temptation."

She pondered that. "A colleague?"

"That's right. He still works with Micah Steele," he said. "He's a demolitions expert."

"Isn't that dangerous?"

"Very," he replied. "His wife died four years ago. Committed suicide," he added shockingly. "He never got over it."

"Why did she do something so drastic?" she asked.

"Because he was working for the FBI when they married and he got shot a few months after the wedding. She hadn't realized his work would be so dangerous. He was in the hospital for weeks and she went haywire. He wouldn't give up a job he loved, and she found that she couldn't live with the knowledge that he might end up dead. She couldn't give him up, either, so she took what she considered the easy way out." His face set grimly. "Easy for her. Hell on him."

She drew in a sharp breath. "I suppose he felt guilty."

"Yes. That was about the time Maggie broke up with me," he added. "She said she didn't want to end up like Patricia."

"She knew Cord's wife?"

"They were best friends," he said shortly. "And something happened between Cord and Maggie just after Mrs. Barton's funeral. I never knew what, but it ended in Maggie's sudden marriage to a man old enough to be her father. I don't know why, but I think it had something to do with Cord."

"He's unique."

He glared at her. "Yes. He's a hardened mercenary now. He gave up law enforcement when Patricia died and took a job with an ex-special forces unit that went into freelance work. He started doing demolition work and now it's all he does."

Her eyes softened. "He wants to die."

"You're perceptive," he mused. "That's what I think, too. Hell of a pity that he and Maggie don't see each other. They're a lot alike."

She looked at her purse. "You aren't still carrying a torch for her?"

He chuckled. "No. She's a kind, sweet woman and I probably would have married her if things had been different. But I don't think she could have lived with me. She takes things too much to heart."

"Don't I?" she fished.

He smiled. "At times. But you're spunky, Miss Johnson, and despite the scare you had with your two neighbors, you don't balk at fighting back. I like your spirit. When I lose my temper, and I do occasionally, you won't be looking for a closet to hide in."

"That might be true," she confessed. "But if you were into demolition work, I think I'd run in the opposite direction when I saw you coming."

He nodded. "Which is exactly what Maggie did," he replied. "She ran from Cord and got engaged to me."

That was heartening. If the woman was carrying a torch for another man, it might stop Eb from falling back into his old relationship with her.

"Jealous?" he murmured with a sensuous glance.

Her heart raced. She moved one shoulder a little and avoided his eyes. Then she sighed and said, "Yes."

He chuckled. "Now that really is flattering," he said. "Maggie is part of the past. I have no hidden desire to rekindle old flames. Except the one you and I shared," he qualified.

Sally turned her head and met his searching gaze. Her breath caught in her throat as she stared back at him hungrily.

"Watch it," he said, not quite jokingly. "When we drive up in your yard, we'll be under surveillance. I don't want an audience for what we were doing in the parking lot at that restaurant."

She laughed delightedly. "Okay."

"On the other hand," he added, "we could find a deserted road."

She hesitated. It was one thing for it to happen spontaneously, but quite another to plan such a sensual interlude. And she wasn't sure of her own protective instincts. Around Eb, she didn't seem to have any.

"Don't make such heavy weather of it," he said after a minute. "There's no hurry. We've got all the time in the world."

"Have we?" she wondered, remembering Lopez and his threats.

"Don't gulp down your life, Sally," he said. "Take it one minute at a time. I'm not going to let anything happen to you or Jessica or Stevie. Okay?"

She swallowed. "Sorry. I panic when I think about how dangerous it is."

"I've been handling danger for a long time," he reminded her. "I have a state-of-the-art surveillance system. Nothing is going to get past it."

She managed a weak smile. "He's very ruthless."

"He's been getting away with murder," he said simply. "He doesn't think the justice system can touch him. We're going to prove to him that it can."

"How do you bring a man to justice when he's rich enough to buy a country?"

"You cut off the source of his wealth," he said simply. "Without its head, the snake can't go far."

"Good point."

"Now stop worrying."

"I'll try."

He reached across the seat for her hand and locked it into his big, warm one. "I enjoyed tonight."

"So did I," she said gently.

"Maggie isn't my future, in case you were wondering," he added in a soft tone.

Sally hoped fervently that it was true. She wanted Eb with all her heart.

His fingers tightened on hers. "I think it might be a good idea if I start driving you and Stevie to school and picking you up in the afternoons."

Her heart leaped. "Why?"

He glanced at her. "Because Lopez wouldn't hesitate to kidnap either or both of you to further his own ends. Even two miles is a long distance when you don't have any sort of protection."

She stared at him worriedly. "Why didn't Jess leave well enough alone?" she asked miserably. "If she hadn't gotten that person to talk…"

"Hindsight is wonderful," he told her. "But try to remember that Lopez's operation supplies about a quarter of all narcotics sold in the States. That's a lot of addicted kids and a fair number of dead ones."

She grimaced. "Sorry. I was being selfish."

"It isn't selfish to be concerned for the welfare of people you love," he told her. "But getting Lopez behind bars, and cutting his connections, will help make the world a better place. A little worry isn't such a bad trade-off, considering."

"I guess not."

He brought the back of her hand to his mouth and kissed it warmly. "You looked lovely tonight," he said. "I was proud of you."

Her face flushed at the rare compliment. "I'm always proud of you," she replied softly.

He chuckled. "You're good for my ego."

"You're good for mine."

He kept his eyes on the road with an effort. He wanted to pull the car onto a side road and make passionate love to her, but that was impractical, given the circumstances. All Lopez's men needed was an opportunity. He wasn't going to give them one, despite his teasing comment to Sally about it.

When they pulled up in her driveway, the lights were all on in the house and Dallas was sitting in the front porch swing, smoking like a furnace.

"Have a nice time?" he asked as Eb and Sally came up the steps.

"Very nice," Eb replied. "I ran into Cord Romero."

"I thought he was overseas, helping detonate unexploded land mines?"

"Not now," Eb told him. "He's in Houston. Between jobs, maybe. Why are you sitting out here?"

Dallas stared at the red tip of his cigarette. "Jessica has a cough," he replied. "I didn't want to aggravate it."

"Are the two of you speaking?" Eb drawled.

Dallas laughed softly. "Well, she's stopped trying to throw things at me, at least."

Sally's eyes went enormous. That didn't sound like her staid aunt.

"What was she throwing?" Eb asked.

"Anything within reach that felt expendable," came the dry reply. "Stevie thought it was great fun, but she wouldn't let him play. He's gone to bed. She's pretending to watch television."

"You might talk to her," Eb suggested.

"Chance," Dallas replied, "would be a fine thing. She

doesn't want to talk, thank you.'' He finished the cigarette.
''I'll be out in the woods with Smith.''

''Watch where you walk,'' Eb cautioned.

''Mined the forest, did we?'' Dallas murmured wickedly.

Eb grinned. ''Not with explosives, at least.''

Dallas shook his head and went down the steps, to vanish in the direction of the woods at the edge of the yard.

Sally rubbed her arms through the coat, shivering, and it wasn't even that cold. She felt the danger of her predicament keenly and wished that she could have done something to prevent the desperate situation.

''You're doing it again,'' Eb murmured, drawing her against him. ''You have to trust me. I won't let anything happen to any of you.''

She looked up at him with wide, soft eyes. ''I'll try not to worry. I've never been in such a mess before.''

''Hopefully you never will again,'' he said. He bent and kissed her very gently, nipping her lower lip before he lifted his head. ''I'll be somewhere nearby, or my men will be. Try to get some sleep.''

''Okay.'' She touched her fingers to his mouth and smiled wanly before she turned and walked to the door. ''Thanks for supper,'' she added. ''It was delicious.''

''It would have been better without the company,'' he said, ''but that was unavoidable. Next time I'll plan better.''

She smiled at him. ''That's a deal.''

He watched her walk inside the house and lock the door behind her before he turned and got back into his truck. Less than twenty-four hours remained before Lopez would make good his threat. He had to make sure that everyone was prepared for a siege.

* * *

Sally paused in the doorway of the living room with her eyes wide as she saw the damage Jessica had inflicted with her missiles.

"Good Lord!" she exclaimed.

Jess grimaced. "Well, he provoked me," she muttered. "He said that I'd gotten lazy in my old age, just lying around the house like a garden slug. I do not lie around like a garden slug!"

"No, of course you don't," Sally said, placating her while she bent to pick up pieces of broken pottery and various other objects from the floor.

"Besides, what does he expect me to do without my eyesight, drive the car?"

Sally was trying not to smile. She'd never seen her aunt in such a tizzy before.

"He actually accused me of insanity because I won't give up the name to Lopez," she added harshly. "He said that a good mother wouldn't have withheld a name and put her child in danger. That's when I threw the flowerpot, dear. I'm sorry. I do hope it hit him."

Sally made a clucking sound. "You're not yourself, Jess."

"Yes, I am! I'm the result of all his sarcasm! He can't find one thing about me that he likes anymore. Everything I do and say is wrong!"

"He doesn't seem like a bad man," Sally ventured.

"I didn't say he was bad, I said he was obnoxious and condescending and conceited." She pushed back a strand of hair. "He was laughing the whole time."

Which surely made things worse, Sally mused silently. "I expect it was wails of pain, Jess."

"You couldn't hurt him," she scoffed. "You'd have to stick a bomb up his shirt."

"Drastic surely?"

Jess sighed and leaned back in the chair, looking drained. "I hate arguments. He seems to thrive on them." She hesitated. "He taught Stevie how to braid a rope," she added unexpectedly.

"That's odd. I thought Stevie wanted to beat him up."

"They had a talk outside the room. I don't know what was said," Jess confessed. "But when they came back in here, Dallas had several lengths of rawhide and he taught Stevie how to braid them. He was having the time of his life."

"Then what?"

"Then," she said, her lips compressing briefly, "he just happened to mention that I could have taught him how to braid rope and a lot of other things if I'd exert myself occasionally instead of vegetating in front of a television that I can't see anyway."

"I see."

"Pity I ran out of things to throw," she muttered. "I was reaching for the lamp when he called a draw and said he was going to sit on the front porch. Then Stevie decided to go to bed." She gripped the arms of her chair hard. "Everybody ran for cover. You'd think I was a Chinese rocket or something."

"In a temper, there is something of a comparison," Sally chuckled.

The older woman drew in a long breath. "Anyway, how was your date?"

"Not bad. We ran into his ex-fiancée at the restaurant."

"Maggie?" Jess asked, wide-eyed. "How is she?"

"She's very pretty and still crazy about Eb, from all indications. I think she'd have followed us home if her dark and handsome escort hadn't half dragged her away."

"Cord was there?"

"You know him?" Sally asked curiously.

Jess nodded. "He was a handsome devil. I had a yen for him once myself, but he married Patricia instead. She was a little Dresden china doll, blonde and absolutely gorgeous. She worshipped Cord. They'd only been married a few months when he was involved in a shoot-out with a narcotics dealer. She couldn't take it. When Cord came home from the hospital, she was several days dead, with a suicide note clutched in her fingers. He found her. He was like a madman after that, looking for every dangerous job he could find. I don't suppose he's over her yet. He loved her desperately."

"Eb says he works with Micah Steele."

"He does, and there's a real coincidence. Micah also has a stepsister, Callie. You know her, she works in Mr. Kemp's law office."

"Yes. We went to school together. But Micah doesn't have anything to do with her or his father since his father divorced Callie's mother. They say," she murmured, "that old Mr. Steele caught Micah with his new wife in a very compromising position and tossed them both out on their ears."

"That's the obvious story," Jessie said dryly. "But there's more to it than that."

"How does Callie feel about Micah's work, do you think?"

"The way any woman would feel," Jessie replied gently. "Afraid."

Sally knew that Jess was talking about Dallas, and how she'd regarded his work as a soldier of fortune. She stared at the darkened window, wondering how she'd feel under the same circumstances. At least Eb wasn't involved in demolition work or actively working as a mercenary. She knew that she could adjust to Eb's lifestyle. But the trick was going to be convincing Eb that she could—and that he needed her, as much as she needed him.

Chapter Nine

Sally found herself jumping at every odd noise all day Saturday. Jessica could feel the tension that she couldn't see.

"You have to trust Eb," she told her niece while Stevie was watching cartoons in the living room. "He knows what he's doing. Lopez won't succeed."

Sally grimaced over her second cup of coffee. Across the kitchen table from her, Jess looked serene. She wished she could feel the same way.

"I'm not worried about us," she pointed out. "It's Stevie…"

"Dallas won't let anything happen to Stevie," came the quiet reply.

Sally smiled, remembering the broken objects in the living room the night before. She drew a lazy circle around the lip of her coffee cup while she searched for the right words. "At least, the two of you are speaking."

"Yes. Barely," her aunt acknowledged wryly. "But Stevie likes him now. They started comparing statistics on wrestlers. They both like wrestling, you see. Dallas knows all sorts of holds. He wrestled on his college team.''

''Wrestling!'' Sally chuckled.

''Apparently there's a lot more to the professional matches than just acting ability,'' Jessica said dryly. ''I'm finding it rather interesting, even if I can't see what they're doing. They explained the holds to me.''

''Common threads,'' Sally murmured.

''And one stitch at a time. What did you think of Cord Romero?''

''He's the strangest ex-schoolteacher I've ever met,'' Sally said flatly.

''He was never cut out for that line of work,'' Jessica said, sipping black coffee. ''But demolition work isn't much of a profession, either. Pity. He'll be two lines of type on the obituary page one day, and it's such a waste.''

''Eb says Maggie's running from him.''

''Relentlessly,'' Jess said dryly. ''I always thought she got engaged to Eb just to shake Cord up, but it didn't work. He doesn't see her.''

''He's in the same line of work Eb was,'' Sally pointed out, ''and Eb said that his job was why she called off the wedding.''

''I think she just came to her senses. If you love a man, you don't have a lot to say about his profession if it's a long-standing one. Cord's wife was never cut out for life on the edge. Maggie, now, once had a serious run-in with a couple of would-be muggers. She had a big flashlight in her purse and she used it like a mace.'' She laughed softly. ''They both had to have stitches before they went off to jail. Cord laughed about it for weeks afterward. No, she had the strength to marry Eb—she simply didn't love him.''

Sally traced the handle of her cup. "Eb says he isn't carrying a torch for her."

"Why should he be?" she asked. "She's a nice woman, but he never really loved her. He wanted stability and he thought marriage would give it to him. As it turned out, he found his stability after a bloody firefight in Africa, and it was right here in Jacobsville."

"Do you think he'll ever marry?" she fished.

"When he's ready," Jess replied. "But I don't think it will be Maggie. Just in case you wondered," she teased.

Sally pushed back a wisp of hair from her eyes. "Jess, do you know where your informant is now, the one that Lopez wants you to name?"

She shook her head. "We lost touch just after Lopez was arrested. I understand that my informant went back to Mexico. I haven't tried to contact...the person."

"What if the informant betrays himself?"

"You're clutching at straws, dear," Jessica said gently. "That isn't going to happen. And I'm not giving a witness up to the executioner in cold blood even to save myself and my family."

Sally smiled. "No. I know you wouldn't. I wouldn't, either. But it's scary to be in this situation."

"It is. But it will be over one day, and we'll get back to normal. Whatever happens, happens." Jess reminded her niece, "It's like that old saying, when your time's up, it's up. We may not know what we're doing, but God always does. And He doesn't have tunnel vision."

"Point taken. I'll try to stop worrying."

"You should. Eb is one of the best in the world at what he does. Lopez knows it, too. He won't rush in headfirst, despite his threat."

"What if he has a missile launcher?" Sally asked with sudden fear.

Miles away in a communications hot room, a man with green eyes nodded his head and shot an order to a subordinate. It wouldn't hurt one bit to check out the intelligence for that possibility. Sally might be nervous, but she had good instincts. And a guardian angel in cowboy boots.

Manuel Lopez was a small man with big ambition. He was nearing forty, balding, cynical and mercenary to the soles of his feet. He stared out the top floor picture window of his four-story mansion at the Gulf of Mexico and cursed. One of his subordinates, shifting nervously from one foot to the other, had just brought him some unwelcome news and he was livid.

"There are only a handful of men," the subordinate said in quiet Spanish. "Not a problem if we send a large force against them."

Lopez turned and glared at the man from yellow-brown eyes. "Yes, and if we send a large force, the FBI and the DEA will also send a large force!"

"It would be too late by then," the man replied with a shrug.

"I have enough federal problems in the United States as it is," Lopez growled. "I do not anticipate giving them an even better reason to send an undercover unit after me here! Scott has influence with his government. I want the name of the informant, not to wade in and kill the woman and her protectors."

The other man stared at the spotless white carpet. "She will never give up the name of her informant," he said simply. "Not even for the sake of her child."

Lopez turned fully to look at the man. "Because now it is only words, the threat. We must make it very real, you understand? At midnight tonight in Jacobsville, precisely at midnight, you will have a helicopter fly over the house and drop a smoke bomb. A big one." His eyes narrowed and he smiled. "This will be the attack they anticipate. But not the real one, you understand?"

"They will probably have missiles," the man said quietly.

"And they are far too soft to use them," came the sneering reply. "This is why we will ultimately win. I have no scruples. Now, listen. I will want a man to remove one of the elementary school janitors. He can be drugged or threatened, I have no interest in the method, just get him out of the way for one day. Then you will have one of our men take his place. The substitute must know what the child looks like and which class he is in. He is to be taken very covertly, so that nothing out of the way is projected until it is too late and we have him. You understand?"

"Yes," the man replied respectfully. "Where is he to be held?"

Lopez smiled coldly. "At the rental house near the Johnson home," he said. "Will that not be an irony to end all ironies?" His eyes darkened. "But he is not to be harmed. That must be made very clear," he added in tones that chilled. "You remember what happened to the man who went against my orders and set fire to my enemy's house in Wyoming without waiting for the man to be alone, and a five-year-old boy was killed?"

The other man swallowed and nodded quickly.

"If one hair on this boy's head is harmed," he added, "I will see to it that the man responsible fares even worse than his predecessor. I am a violent man, but I do not kill children. It is, perhaps, my only virtue." He waved his hand. "Let me know when my orders have been carried out."

"Yes. At once."

He watched the man go and his odd yellow-brown eyes

narrowed. He had watched his mother and siblings die at the hands of a guerrilla leader at the age of four. His father had been a poor laborer who could barely earn enough to provide one meal a day for the two of them, so his childhood had been spent scavaging for food like an animal, hiding in the shadows to avoid being tortured by the invaders. His father had not been as fortunate, but the two of them had managed to work their way to the States, to Victoria, Texas, when he was ten. He watched his father scrape and bow as a janitor and hated the sight. He had vowed that when he was a man, he would never know poverty again, regardless of what it cost him. And despite his father's anguish, he had embarked very quickly on a path to easy money.

He looked down at the white carpet, a dream of his from youth, and at the wealth with which he surrounded himself. He dealt in drugs and death. He was wealthy and immensely powerful. A word from him could topple heads of state. But it was an empty, cold, bitter existence. He had lived at first only for vengeance, for the ability and the means to avenge his mother and his baby brother and sister. That accomplished, he wanted wealth and power. One step led to another, until he was in over his head, first as a murderer, then as a thief, and finally, as a drug lord. He was ruthless and he knew that one day his sins would catch up with him, but first he was going to know who had sold him out to the authorities two years before. What irony that vengeance had led him to power, and now it was vengeance that had almost brought him down. He cursed the woman Jessica for refusing to give him the name. He had only discovered her part in his arrest six months before. She would pay now. He would have the name of his betrayer, whatever the cost!

He stared down at the rocks and winced as he saw once

again, in his memory, the floating white dress and the equally white face and open, dead eyes of the woman he'd wanted even more than the name of the person who had betrayed him. Isabella, he thought with anguish. He had never loved, not until Isabella came into his home as a housekeeper, the sister of one of his lieutenants' friends. She had talked to him, admired him, teased him as if he were a boy. She had made herself so necessary to him that he told her things that he told no one else. She had made him want to be clean, to give up his decadent life, to have a family, a home. But when he had approached her ardently, she had suddenly wanted no part of him. In a fit of rage when she pushed him away at a party on his yacht, he hit her. She went over the rails and into the ocean, vanishing abruptly under the keel of the boat.

He had immediately regretted the act, but it was too late. His men had searched for her in the water until daybreak before he let them give up the search, only to find her washed up on the beach, dead, when he arrived back at his mansion. Her death had cheapened him, cheapened his life. He was deeply sorry that his temper had pushed him to such an act, that he cost himself the most precious thing in his life. He had killed her. He was damned, he thought. Damned eternally. And probably he deserved to be.

Since that night, two years ago, just before his arrest in the United States for narcotic trafficking, he had no other thought than to find the man who had betrayed him. Nothing made him happy since her loss, not even the pretty young woman who sang at a club in Cancún just recently. He had taken a fancy to her because she reminded him of Isabella. He had ordered his henchmen to bring her to him one night after her performance. He had enjoyed her, but her violent revulsion had angered him and she, too, had felt his wrath. She had taken her own life, jumped from a high balcony rather than submit to him a second time. Her death had wounded him, but not as deeply as the loss of Isabella. Nothing, he was certain, would ever give him such anguish and remorse again. He thought of the woman Jessica and her son, of the fear she would experience when he had her child. Then, he thought angrily, she would give him the name of her informant. She would have to. And, at last, he would have his vengeance for the betrayal that had sent him to an American prison.

Eb hadn't come near the house all day. After Stevie was tucked up in bed, Jessica and Sally sat together in the dimly lit living room and watched the clock strike midnight.

"It's time," Sally said huskily, stiff with nerves.

Jessica only nodded. Like Sally, her frame was rigid. She had made her decision, the only decision possible. Now they were all going to pay the consequences for it.

Even as the thought crawled through her mind, she heard the sudden whir of a helicopter closing in.

"Get down!" Jessica called to Sally, sliding onto the big throw rug full-length. She felt Sally beside her as the helicopter came even closer and a flash, followed by an explosion, shook the roof.

Smoke came down the chimney, filling the room. Outside, the whir of the helicopter was accompanied by small arms fire and the sounds of bullets hitting something hard. Then that sound was abruptly interrupted by a sudden whooshing sound. Right on the heels of that came a violent explosion that lit up the whole sky and then the unmistakable sound of falling debris.

"There went the chopper," Jessica said huskily. "Sally, are you all right?"

"Yes. We have to get out," she said, coughing. "The smoke is going to choke us!"

She helped Jessica to her feet and started her down the hall to the front door while she went to grab Stevie up out of his bed and rush down the same hall with him in her arms. It was like a nightmare, but she didn't have time to count the cost or worry about the outcome. She was doing what was necessary to save them, in the quickest possible time. She could only pray that they wouldn't run out right into the arms of Lopez's men.

She caught up with Jess, who was feeling her way along the wall. Taking her by the arm, with Stevie close, she propelled them to the front door, unlocked it, and rushed out onto the porch.

Eb was running toward them, but an Eb that Sally didn't recognize at first. He was dressed completely in black with a face mask on, carrying a small automatic weapon. Other men, similarly dressed, were already going around the back of the house.

"Come with me," Eb called, herding them into the forest and into a four-wheel-drive vehicle. "Lock the doors and stay put until we check out the house," he said.

He was gone even as the words died on the air. Stevie huddled close to his mother while Sally watched Eb's stealthy but rapid approach toward the house, her heart racing madly. Even though the attack had been expected, it was frightening.

A tap on the window next to Jessica on the passenger side made them all jump. Dallas pulled off his face mask, smiling as he replaced a walkie-talkie in his belt. "Open the window," he said.

Sally fumbled with the key in the ignition and powered the passenger side window down.

"We got the chopper," he said. "But it's only a smoke

bomb in the house, irritating but not deadly. Lopez is a man of his word. He did attack at midnight. Pity about the chopper," he added with glittery eyes. "That will set him back a little small change."

Sally didn't ask the obvious question, but she knew that somebody had to be piloting that helicopter. She felt sick inside, now that the danger was past.

"Is everyone all right?" Jessica asked. "We heard shots."

"The chopper was well-equipped with weapons," Dallas said. "But he wasn't a very good shot."

"Thank God," Jessica said heavily.

Dallas reached in and touched her face gently, pausing to run a rough hand over Stevie's tousled hair. "Don't be afraid," he said softly. "I won't let anything happen to you."

Jessica held his hand to her cheek and choked back a sob. Dallas bent to touch his mouth to her wet eyes.

Impulsively Stevie leaned across his mother to hug the big blond man, too. Watching them, Sally felt empty and alone. They were already a family, even if they hadn't realized it.

Dallas's walkie-talkie erupted in a burst of static. "All clear," Eb's voice came back to them. "I'm phoning the sheriff while the others open the windows and turn on the attic fan to get this smoke out of here. Then I'll lock up."

"What about…" Dallas began.

"We'll take the women and Stevie home with us," he said. "No sense in leaving them here for the rest of the night. Sally?"

Dallas moved the walkie-talkie to her mouth. "Yes?" she said, shaken.

"Come in and help me find what you need in the way

of clothes for all three of you. Dallas, take Jess and Stevie back to the house. We'll catch up.''

"Sure thing."

Sally got out of the vehicle, still in her jeans and sneakers and sweatshirt, her long hair falling out of its braid. Dallas got in under the wheel as she walked back to the house. She heard the engine roar and glanced back to see the utility vehicle pull out of the yard. At least Jess and Stevie were safe. But she felt shaken to the soles of her sneakers.

Eb was in the smoky living room, having just hung up the phone. His mask was in one hand, dangling along with the small machine gun. He looked tough and angry as he glanced at Sally's white face. He didn't say a word. He just held out his arm.

Sally ran to him, and he gathered her up in his arms and held her tight while she shivered from the shock of it all.

"I'm no wimp, honest," she whispered in a choked attempt at humor. "But I'm not used to people bombing my house."

He chuckled deeply and hugged her close. "Only a smoke bomb, baby," he said gently. "Noisy and frightening, but not dangerous unless it set fire to something. He had to make a statement, you see. Lopez is a man of his word."

"Damn Lopez," she muttered.

"Amen."

Around them, men were pouring over the house. Eb escorted Sally down the hall to her bedroom.

"Get what you need together," he said, "but only essentials. I'd like to get you out of here very soon after the sheriff arrives."

"The sheriff...?"

"It's his jurisdiction," he told her. "I'm sanctioned, if

that's what the worried look is about,'' he added when he saw her face. He smiled. "I wouldn't take the law into my own hands. Not in this country, anyway," he added with a grin.

"Thank goodness," she said heavily. "I had visions of trying to bail you out of jail."

"Would you?" he teased.

"Of course."

She looked so solemn that the smile faded from his lips. He gathered a handful of her thick blond hair and pulled her wan face under his. His grip was a little tight, and the look in his green eyes was glittery. "Danger is an aphrodisiac, did you know?" he whispered roughly, and bent to her mouth.

He hadn't kissed her that way before. His mouth was hard and demanding on her lips, parting them ruthlessly as his body shifted and one arm pushed her hips deliberately into the changing contours of his own.

She felt helpless. Her mouth opened for him. Her body arched up, taut and hot, in the grip of madness. She returned his kiss ardently, moaning when his legs parted so that he could maneuver her hips between them, letting her feel the power of his arousal.

His tall, fit body shuddered and she could feel the sharp indrawn breath he took.

After a few wild seconds, he dragged his mouth away from hers without letting her move away even a fraction of an inch. He looked down at her with intent, searching her wide, soft gray eyes hungrily. The arm that was holding her was like a steel rod at her back, but against her legs, she felt the faintest tremor in his.

"I've gone hungry for a long time," he whispered gruffly.

She didn't know how to reply to such a blatant statement. Her eyes searched his in an odd silence, broken only by the whir of the attic fan in the hall and the muffled sound of voices as Eb's men searched the house. She reached up and touched his hard mouth tenderly, loving the immediate response of his lips to the caress.

He bent, nuzzling his face against hers to find her mouth. He kissed her urgently, but with restraint, nibbling her lower lip sensuously. Both arms went around her, riveting her to him. Her own slid under his arms and around his hard waist, holding him close. She closed her eyes, savoring the wondrous contact. The fierce hunger he felt was quite obvious in the embrace, but it didn't frighten her. She wanted him, too.

"When I heard the explosion," he said at her ear, his voice tight with tension, "I didn't know what we were going to find when I ran toward the house. We'd planned for any eventuality, but the chopper came in under radar. We didn't even hear the damned thing until we could see it, and then the launcher jammed...!"

She hadn't imagined that Eb would be afraid for her. It was wonderful. She hugged him closer and felt him shiver.

"We were a little shaken," Sally whispered. "But we're all okay."

"I didn't expect to feel like this," he said through his teeth.

She lifted her head and looked up at his strained face. "Like...this?"

His green gaze met her soft gray one and then fell to her mouth, to her soft breasts flattened against him. "Like this," he whispered and moved deliberately against her while he held her eyes.

She blushed, because it was blatant.

But he didn't smile. "I knew you were going to be trouble six years ago," he said through his teeth. He bent and kissed her again, fiercely, before he put her away from him and stood trying to get his breath.

She was shivering a little in the aftermath of the most explosive sensuality she'd ever felt. She searched his face quietly, despite the turmoil inside her awakened body.

"You've never felt like that before, have you?" he asked in a hushed tone.

She shook her head, still too shaken for words.

"If it's any consolation, it gets steadily worse," he continued. "Think about that."

He turned and went out into the hall with her puzzled eyes following him. She touched her swollen lips gingerly and wondered what he meant.

The sheriff, Bill Elliott, and two deputies pulled up in the yard, took statements and looked around with Eb and the other men. Sally was questioned briefly, and when the house was secure, Eb drove her back to his house with the rest of his men remaining in the woods.

"I don't think Lopez has any idea of trying again tonight," he said, "but I'm not taking any chances. I've already underestimated him once."

"He does keep his word," she said huskily.

"Yes."

"What do we do now?"

"I take you and Stevie to school and Jess stays at my house. In fact, you all stay at my house," he said curtly. "I'm not putting you at risk a second time."

She was stunned at the emotion in his voice. He was really concerned about her. She felt a warm glow all the way to her toes.

He glanced at her with slow, sensuous eyes. "At least at my own house, I can find one room with no bugs." His eyes went to her breasts and back to her face. "I'm starving."

She knew he wasn't talking about food, and her heart began racing madly.

He caught her hand in his free one and worked his fingers slowly between hers, pressing her palm to his. "Don't worry. I won't let things go too far, Sally."

She wasn't worried about that. She was wondering how she was going to go on living if he made love to her and then walked away.

When they got to the house, Jessica and Dallas were in the small bedroom Eb's male housekeeper had given Stevie, tucking him in.

Eb had his housekeeper show the others to their rooms and he excused himself, tugging Sally along with him, to Dallas's obvious amusement.

"Where are we going?" Sally asked.

"To bed. I'm tired. Aren't you?"

"Yes."

She supposed he was giving her a room further down the hall, but he didn't stop at any of the closed doors. He led her around a corner and through two double doors into a huge room with Mediterranean furnishings and green and gold and brown accessories. He closed the double doors, locking them, before he turned to the dresser and pulled out a pair of blue silk pajamas.

"You can wear the pajama top and I'll wear the bottoms," he said matter-of-factly.

Her breath escaped in a rush. "Eb…"

He drew her into his arms and kissed her slowly, with deliberate sensuality, making nonsense of her protests with his hands as they skimmed under the sweatshirt and up to find her taut breasts.

She moaned, feeling the fever rise in her as he unfastened the bra and touched her hungrily. Her body arched, helping him, inviting him. Her hands gripped hard against the powerful muscles of his upper arms, drowning in waves of pleasure.

His mouth lifted fractionally. "I won't hurt you," he breathed. "Not in any way. But you're sleeping in my arms tonight."

She started to protest, but his mouth was already covering hers, muffling the words, muffling her brain.

His hands removed the sweatshirt and the bra and he looked at her with quiet, possessive eyes, drinking in the soft textures, the smooth skin, the beauty of her. He touched her gently, smiling as her body reacted to his skilled hands.

His mouth slid down to her breasts and kissed them slowly, each caress more ardent than the one before. He had her out of her jeans and sneakers and down to her briefs before she realized what was happening,

He moved away just long enough to pick up the pajama top and slip it over her head, still buttoned. He lifted her, dazed, in his arms and paused, balancing her on one knee, to pull the covers back so that he could tuck her into bed. He leaned over her, balancing on his hands, and searched her flushed, fascinated face.

"I'll be in after I've talked to Dallas and reset the monitors."

She didn't bother to protest. Her gray eyes searched his and she sighed a little unsteadily. "All right."

His eyes kindled with pleasure. He smiled, because he knew she was accepting anything he proposed. It was humbling. He kissed her eyelids closed. "Sleep well."

She watched him go, uncertain if that meant he was sleeping elsewhere. She was so tired that she fell asleep almost as soon as the doors closed behind him, wrapped in sensuous dreams.

Chapter Ten

Sally had violent, passionate dreams that night. She moved helplessly under invisible caressing hands, moaning, arching up to prolong their warm, sweet contact. Her body burned, swelled, ached. She whispered to some faceless phantom, pleading with it not to stop.

There was soft, deep laughter at her ear and the rough warmth of an unshaven face moving against her skin, where her heart beat frantically. Slowly it occurred to her that it felt just a little too vivid to be a dream…

Her eyes flew open and blond-streaked brown hair came into focus under them in the pale dawn light filtering in through the window curtains. Her hands were enmeshed in its thick, cool strands and when she looked down, she realized that her pajama top was open, baring her to a marauding mouth.

"Eb!" she exclaimed huskily.

"It's all right. You're only dreaming," he whispered, and his mouth slid up to cover her lips as the hair-roughened skin of his muscular chest slid over her bare breasts. She felt his legs entwining with her own, felt the throb of his body, the tenderness of his hands, his mouth, as he learned her by touch and taste.

"Dreaming?"

"That's right." He lifted his lips from hers and looked down into misty gray eyes. He smiled. "And a lovely dream it is," he added in a whisper as he lifted away enough to give his eyes a stark view of everything the pajama top no longer covered. "Lovelier than I ever imagined."

"What time is it?" she asked, dazed.

"Dawn," he told her, smoothing her long hair back away from her flushed face. "Everyone else is still asleep. And there are no bugs, of any sort, in here with us," he added meaningfully.

She touched his rough cheek gently, studying him as he'd studied her. He was still wearing the pajama trousers, but his broad chest was bare. Like her own.

He rolled over onto his back, taking her with him. He guided her hands to his chest with a quiet smile. "I was going to let you wake up alone," he murmured. "But I didn't have enough willpower. There you lay, blond hair scattered over my pillows, the pajama top half off." He shook his head. "You can't imagine how lovely you look in the dawn light. Like a fairy, all creamy and gold. Irresistible," he added, "to a man who's abstained as long as I have."

She traced the pattern of hair over his breastbone. "How long have you abstained?"

"Years too long," he whispered, searching her eyes. "And that's why I set the alarm in Dallas's room to go off five minutes from now. It will wake him and he'll wake Jess and Stevie. Stevie will come looking for you." He grinned. "See how carefully I look after your virtue, Miss Johnson?"

She gave her own bare torso a poignant glance and met his eyes again.

He lifted an eyebrow. "Virtue," he emphasized, "not modesty. I don't seduce virgins, in case you forgot."

She couldn't quite decide whether he was playing or serious.

He saw that in her face and smiled gently. "Sally, the hardest thing I ever did in my life was to push you away one spring afternoon six years ago," he said softly. "I had passionate, vivid dreams about you in some of the wildest places on earth. I'm still having them." His hand swept slowly down her body, watching it lift helplessly to his touch. "So are you, judging by the sounds you were making in your sleep when I came to bed about ten minutes ago. I crawled in beside you and you came right up against me and touched me in a way I won't tell you about."

She searched his eyes blankly. "I did what?"

"Want to know?" he asked with an outrageous grin. "Okay." He leaned close and whispered it in her ear and she cried out, horrified.

"No need to feel embarrassed," he chided. "I loved it."

She knew her face was scarlet, but he looked far more pleased than teasing.

He traced her lower lip lazily. "For a few tempestuous seconds I forgot Lopez and last night, and just about everything else of any immediate importance." His eyes darkened as he held her poised above him. "I've lived on dreams for a long time. The reality is pretty shattering."

"Dreams?"

He nodded. He wasn't smiling. "I wanted you six years ago. I still do, more than ever." He brushed back her disheveled hair and looked at her with eyes that were tender and possessive. "I'm your home. Wherever I go, you go."

She didn't understand what he meant. Her face was troubled.

He rolled her over onto her back and propped himself above her. "From what I know of you, my life-style isn't going to break you. You've got spirit and courage, and you're not afraid to speak your mind. I think you'll adjust very well, especially if I give up any work that takes me out of the country. I can still teach tactics, although I'll cut down my contract jobs when the babies start coming along."

"Babies?" She looked completely blank.

"Listen, kid," he murmured dryly, "what we're doing causes them." He frowned. "Well, not exactly what we're doing. But if we were wearing less, and doing a little more than we're doing, we'd be causing them."

Her whole body tingled. She searched his eyes with a feeling of unreality. "You want to have a child with me?" she asked, awed.

"Oh, yes. I want to have a lot of children with you," he whispered solemnly.

She laid her hands flat on his broad chest, savoring its muscular warmth as she considered what he was saying. She frowned, because he hadn't mentioned love or marriage.

"What's missing?" he asked.

"I teach school," she said worriedly. "My reputation..."

Now he was frowning. "God Almighty, do you think I'm asking you to live in sin with me, in Jacobsville, Texas?" he asked, with exaggerated horror.

"You didn't say anything about marriage," she began defensively.

He grinned wickedly. "Do you really think I spent so much time on you just to give you karate lessons?" he drawled. "Darlin', it would take years of them to make you proficient enough to protect yourself from even a weak adversary. I brought you over here for practice so that I could get my arms around you."

Her eyes brightened. "Did you, really?"

He chuckled. "See what depths I've sunk to?" he murmured. He shook his head. "I had to give you enough time to grow up. I didn't want a teenager who was hero worshiping me. I wanted a woman, a strong woman, who could stand up to me."

She smoothed her hands up to his broad shoulders. "I think I can do that," she mused.

He nodded. "I think you can, too. Can you live with what I do?"

She smiled. "Of course."

He drew in a slow breath and his eyes were more possessive than ever. "Then we'll get Jess out of harm's way and then we'll get married."

She pulled him down to her. "Yes," she whispered against his hard mouth.

Seconds later, they were so close that she wasn't certain he'd be able to draw back at all, when there was a loud knock at the door and the knob rattled.

"Aunt Sally!" came a plaintive little voice. "I want some cereal and they haven't got any that's in shapes and colors. It's such boring cereal!"

Sally laughed even as Eb managed to drag himself away from the tangle of their legs with a groan that was half amusement and half agony.

"I'll be right there, Stevie!"

"Why's the door locked?" he called loudly.

"Come on here, youngster, and let's see if we can find

something you'd like to eat," came a deep, amused adult voice.

"Okay, Dallas!"

The voices retreated. Eb lay shivering a little with reaction, but he grinned when Sally sat up and looked down at him with love glowing in her eyes.

"Close call," he whispered.

"Very," she agreed.

He took a long, hungry last look at her breasts and resolutely sat up and fastened her buttons again with a rueful smile. "Maybe food is a bearable substitute for what I really want," he mused.

She leaned forward and kissed him gently. "I'll make you glad we waited," she whispered against his mouth.

Several heated minutes later, they joined the others at the breakfast table, but Eb didn't mention future plans. He was laying down ground rules for the following week, starting with the very necessary trip Sally and Stevie must take to school the next day.

"We could keep him out of school until this is over," Dallas said tersely, glancing at the child who was sitting between himself and Jessica. "I don't like having him at risk."

"Neither do I," Jessica said heavily. "But it's possible that he won't be. Lopez has a weakness for children," she said. "It's the only virtue he possesses, but he's a maniac about abusive adults. He'd never hurt Stevie, no matter what."

"I'd have to agree with that," Eb said surprisingly.

"Then life goes on as usual," Jessica said. "And maybe Lopez will make a mistake and we'll have him. Or at least," she added, "a way of getting at him."

"What about Rodrigo?" Dallas asked abruptly.

"He phoned me late last night," Eb told him. "He's

already in town, in place. Fast worker. It seems he has a relative, a 'mule' who works for Lopez in Houston, a distant relative who doesn't know what Rodrigo really does for a living. He got Rodrigo a job driving a truck for the new operation here." He let out a breath through his teeth. "Once we get Lopez's attention away from Jess," he added, "that operation is going to be our next priority."

"Can't you just send the sheriff over there to arrest them?" Sally asked.

"It's inside the city limits. Chief Chet Blake has jurisdiction there, and, of course, he'd help if he could," Eb told her. "But so far, all we have on Lopez's employees is a distant connection to a drug lord. Unless we can catch them in the act of receiving or shipping cocaine, what would we charge them with? Building a warehouse is legal, especially when you have all the easements and permission from the planning commission."

"That's why we're going to stake out the place, once this is over," Dallas added. He glanced from Jessica to Stevie with worried eyes. "But first we have to solve the more immediate problem."

Jess felt for his hand on the table beside her and tangled her fingers into it. "We'll get through this," she said in a soft tone. "I can't cold-bloodedly give a human being's life up to Lopez, no matter what the cost. The person involved risked everything to put him away. And even then, his attorneys found a loophole."

"Don't forget that it took them a couple of years to do that," Eb reminded her. "He won't be easy to catch a second time. He has enough pull with the Mexican government to keep them from extraditing him back here for trial."

"I hear DEA's going to put him on their top ten Most Wanted list," Dallas said. "That will turn up the heat a little, especially with a fifty-thousand dollar reward to sweeten the deal.''

"Lopez would double their bounty out of his pocket change to get them off his tail, even if we could find someone crazy enough to go down to Cancún after him," Eb said.

"Micah Steele would, in a second," Dallas replied.

Eb chuckled. "I imagine he would. But he's been working on a case overseas with Cord Romero and Bojo Luciene."

"Bojo, the Moroccan," Dallas recalled. "Now there's a character."

Eb was immediately somber. "Okay, tomorrow morning I'll follow Sally and Stevie in to school. Dallas can tail them on the way home. We'll stay in constant contact and hope for the best."

"The best," Dallas replied, "would be that Lopez would give up."

"It won't happen," Eb assured him.

"Have you considered contacting your informant?" Dallas asked Jessica. "If we could get him back to the States, we could arrange around-the-clock protection and get him into the witness protection program, where even Lopez couldn't find him."

She grimaced. "I thought of that, but I honestly don't know how to locate my informant," she said sadly. "The people who could have helped me do it are dead."

Eb scowled. "All of them?"

Jessica nodded with a sigh. "All of them. About six months ago. Just before my accident."

"Rodrigo might be able to dig something up," Dallas said.

"That's very possible," Eb agreed. "Jessica, you could trust him with the name. I know, you don't want to put your informant in danger. But if we can't find him, how can we protect him?"

She hesitated. Then she shifted in her chair, clinging even more tightly to Dallas's big hand. "Okay," she said finally. "But he has to promise to keep the information to himself. Can I trust him to do that?"

"Yes," Eb said with certainty.

"All right, then. When can we do it?"

"Tomorrow after school," Eb said. "I'll get Cy Parks to run into him 'accidentally' and slip him a note, so that Lopez won't get suspicious."

Jessica's head moved to rest on Dallas's shoulder. "I wish I'd done things differently. So many people at risk, all because I didn't do my job properly."

"But you did," Dallas said at once, sliding a protective arm around her. "You did what any one of us would do. And you did put Lopez away. It's not your fault that he slipped out of the country."

Jessica smiled. "Thanks."

"You going to marry my mama, Dallas?" Stevie piped up.

"Stevie!" Jessica exclaimed.

"Yes, I am," Dallas said, chuckling at Jessica's red face. "She just doesn't know it yet. How do you feel about that, Stevie?"

"That would be great!" he said enthusiastically. "You and me can watch wrestling together!"

"Yes, we can." Dallas kissed Jess's hair gently and looked at his son with proud, possessive eyes.

Sally, watching them, knew that everything was going to be all right for Jessica, once they were out of this mess. She'd be free to marry Eb and she'd never have to worry about her aunt or her cousin again. Even more important, Jessica would be loved. That meant everything to Sally.

Eb followed them to school the next morning, keeping a safe distance. But there were no attempts on them along the way, and once they were inside the building, Sally felt safe. She and Stevie went right along to her class, smiling and greeting teachers and other children they knew.

"It's gonna be all right, isn't it, Aunt Sally?" Stevie asked at the door to her classroom.

"Yes, I think it is," she said with a warm smile.

She checked her lesson plan while the students filed into the classroom. A boy at the back of the room made a face and caught Sally's attention.

"Miss Johnson, there's a puddle of something that smells horrible back here!"

She got up from her desk and went to see. There was, indeed, a puddle. "I'll just go and get one of the janitors," she said with a smile.

But as she started out the door, a tall, quiet man appeared with a mop and pail.

"Hi, Harry," she said to him.

"Hard to be inside today when it's so nice outside," he said with a rueful smile. "I should be sitting on the river in my boat right now."

She smiled. "I'm sorry. But it's a good thing for us that you're here."

He started to wheel the bucket and mop away when one of the wheels came off the bucket. He muttered something and bent to look.

"I'll have to carry it. Can I get one of these youngsters to help me carry the mop?" he asked.

"I'll go!" Stevie volunteered at once.

"Yes, of course," Sally said. "Would you rather I went with you?"

He shook his head. "No need. This strong young man

can manage a mop, can't you, son?'' he asked with a big grin.

"Sure can!" Stevie said, hefting the mop over one shoulder.

"Let's away then, my lad," the man joked. "I'll send him right back, so he won't miss any class," he promised.

"Okay."

She watched Stevie go down the crowded hall behind Harry. It wasn't quite time for class to start, and she didn't think anything of the incident. Until five minutes later, when Stevie hadn't reappeared.

She left a monitor in charge of her class and went down the hall to the janitor's closet. There was the broken bucket, and the mop, but Stevie was nowhere in sight. But the janitor was. He'd been knocked out. She went straight to the office to phone Eb and call the paramedics. Fortunately Harry only had a slight concussion. To be safe, he was taken to the hospital for observation. Sally felt sick. She should have realized that Lopez might send someone to the school. Why had she been so gullible?

Eb arrived at the front office with the police chief, Chet Blake, and two of his officers. They went from door to door, combing the school. But Stevie was no longer there. One of the other janitors remembered seeing a stranger leave the building with the little boy and get into a brown pickup truck in the parking lot.

With that information, the police put out a bulletin. But it was too late. They found the pickup truck minutes later, abandoned in another parking lot, at a grocery store. Stevie was nowhere to be seen.

They waited by the telephone that afternoon for the call that was sure to come. When it did, Eb had to bite down hard on what he wanted to say. Jessica and Sally had been in tears ever since he brought Sally home to the ranch.

"Now," the voice came in a slow, accented drawl, "Stevie's mother will give me the name I want. Or her son will never come home."

"She had to be sedated," Eb said, thinking fast. "She's out cold."

"You have one hour. Not a second longer." The line went dead.

Eb cursed roundly.

"Now what do we do?" Sally asked.

He phoned Cy Parks. "Did you get that message sent for me?" he asked.

"Yes. Scramble the signal."

Eb touched a button on the phone. "Shoot."

Cy gave him a telephone number. "He should be there by now. What can I do to help?"

Eb didn't have to be told that the news about Stevie's abduction was all over town. "Nothing. Wish me luck."

"You know it."

He hung up. Eb dialed the other number and waited. It rang once. Twice. Three times. Four times.

"Come on!" Eb growled impatiently.

On the fifth ring, the receiver was lifted.

"Rodrigo?" Eb asked at once.

"Yes."

"I'm going to put Jessica on the line, and leave the room. She'll give you a name. You know what to do with it."

"Okay."

Eb gave the receiver to Jessica and motioned everybody out of the communications room. He closed the door.

Jessica felt the receiver in her hands and took a deep breath. "The name of my informant was Isabella Medina," she said quietly. "She worked as a housekeeper for..."

There was an intake of breath on the other end of the line. "But surely you knew?" he asked at once.

"Knew what?" Jessica stammered.

"Isabella was found washed up on the rocks in Cancún, just before Lopez's capture," Rodrigo said abruptly. "She is long dead."

"Oh, good Lord," Jessica gasped.

"How could you not know?" he demanded.

Jessica wiped her forehead with a shaking hand. "I lost touch with her just before the trial. I assumed that she'd gone undercover to escape vengeance from Lopez. She wasn't going to testify, after all. She only gave me sources of hard information that I could use to prosecute him. Afterward, there were only three people who knew about her involvement, and they died under rather...mysterious circumstances."

"This is the name Lopez wants?" he asked.

"Yes," she said miserably. "He's got my son!"

"Then you lose nothing by giving him the name," he said quietly. "Do you?"

"No. But he may not even remember her..."

"He was in love with her," Rodrigo said coldly. "His women have a habit of washing up on beaches. The last, a young singer in a Cancún nightclub, died only weeks ago at his hands. There is no proof, of course," he added coldly. "The official cause of death was suicide."

He sounded as though the matter was personal. She hesitated to ask. "You knew the singer?" she ventured.

There was a pause. "Yes. She was...my sister."

"I'm very sorry."

"So am I. Give Lopez the name. It will pacify him and spare your son any more adventures. He will not harm the boy," he added at once. "I think you must know this already."

"I do. At least he has one virtue among so many vices. But it doesn't ease the fear."

"Of course not. Tell Scott I'll be in touch, and not to contact me again. When I have something concrete, I'll call him."

"I'll tell him. Thank you."

"De nada." He hung up.

She went into the other room, feeling her way along the wall.

"Well?" Sally asked.

"My informant is dead," Jessica said sadly. "Lopez killed her, and I never knew. I thought she'd escaped and maybe changed her name."

"What now?" Sally asked miserably.

"I give Lopez the name," Jessica replied. "It will harm no one now. She was so brave. She actually worked in his house and pretended to care about him, just so that she could find enough evidence to convict him. Her father and mother, and her sister, had been gunned down in their village by his men, because they spoke to a government unit about the drug smuggling. She was sick with fear and grief, but she was willing to do anything to stop him." She shook her head. "Poor woman."

"A brave soul," Eb said quietly. "I'm sorry."

"Me, too," Jessica said. She wrapped her arms around herself, feeling chilled. "What if Lopez won't believe me?"

"You know," Eb said quietly, "I think he will."

"Let's hope so," Dallas agreed, his eyes narrow and dark with worry.

Sally put a loving arm around her aunt. "We'll get

Stevie back," she said gently. "Everything's going to be okay."

Jessica hugged her back tearfully. "What would I do without you?" she whispered huskily.

Sally exchanged a long look with Dallas. She smiled. "I think you're going to find out very soon," she teased. "And I'll be your bridesmaid."

"Matron of honor," Eb corrected with soft, tender eyes.

"What?" Jessica exclaimed.

"I'm going to marry your niece, Jess," Eb said gently. "I always meant to, you know. And," he added with mock solemnity, "it does seem the least I can do, considering that she's saved herself for me all these years, despite the blatant temptations of college life…"

"Temptations," Sally chuckled. "If you only knew!"

"Explain that," Eb challenged.

She let go of Jessica and went close to him, sliding her arms naturally around his hard waist. "As if there's a man on the planet who could compare with you," she murmured, and reached up to kiss his chin. Her eyes literally glowed with love. "There never was any competition. There never could be."

Eb lifted an eyebrow. "I could return the compliment," he said in a deep, quiet tone. "You're in a class all your own, Sally mine."

She laid her cheek against his hard chest. "They'll give Stevie back, won't they?" she asked after a minute.

"Yes," he said, utterly certain.

Sally glanced at Jessica, who was close beside Dallas now, leaning against him. They looked as if they'd always belonged together. Things had to turn out all right for them. They just had to. Lopez might have one virtue, but Sally wasn't at all sure that Eb was right. She only prayed that Stevie would be returned when Jess gave up the informant's name. If Lopez did keep his word, and that seemed certain, there was a chance. She had to hope it was a good one.

Chapter Eleven

In exactly an hour from the time Lopez hung up, the phone rang again. Eb let Jessica answer it.

"Hello," she said quietly.

"The name," Lopez replied tersely.

She took a slow breath. "I want you to understand that I would never have given up my informant under ordinary circumstances. But nothing I say can harm her now. I only found out today that she's beyond your vengeance. So it doesn't matter anymore if you know who she was."

"Who...she was?" Lopez asked, his voice hesitant.

"Yes. Was. Her name was Isabella..."

His indrawn breath was so harsh that Jessica almost felt it. "Isabella," he bit off. There was a tense pause. "Isabella."

"I lost touch with her before your trial," Jessica said curtly. "I assumed that she'd gone away and taken on another identity to escape being found out. I didn't know that she was dead already."

Still, Lopez said nothing. The silence went on for so long that Jessica thought the connection was cut.

"Hello?" she asked.

There was another intake of breath. "I loved her," he spat. "In my life, there was no other woman I trusted so much. But she wanted nothing to do with me. I should have known. I should have realized!"

"You killed her, didn't you?" Jessica said coldly.

"Yes," he said, and he didn't sound violent. He sounded oddly subdued. "I never meant to. But I lashed out in a moment's rage, and then it was too late, and all my regrets would not bring her back to life." He drew another breath. "She was close enough to me that she knew things no one else was permitted to know. It occurred to me that she was asking far too many questions, but I was conceited enough to believe she cared for me." There was another brief pause. "The boy will be returned at once. You will find him at the strip mall in the toy store in five minutes. He will not be harmed. You have my word. Nor will you ever be threatened by me again. I...regret...many things," he added in an odd tone, and the line went dead abruptly.

Jessica caught her breath, still holding the receiver in her hand, as if it had life.

"Well?" Dallas asked impatiently.

She felt for the instrument and replaced the receiver with slow deliberation. "He said that Stevie would be in the toy store in the strip mall, in five minutes, unharmed." Her eyes closed. "Unharmed."

Eb motioned Dallas toward Jessica.

"Let's go," he said tersely.

"What if he lied?" Jessica asked as Dallas escorted her out to the big sports utility vehicle Eb drove.

"We both know that Lopez is a man of his word, re-

gardless of his bloody reputation,'' Dallas said tersely.
"We have to hope that he told the truth."

Jessica nibbled on her fingernails all the way to the mall,
which was only about six minutes away from Eb's ranch.
She sat close beside Dallas in the back seat, holding his
hand tightly. Sally glanced back at them, silently praying
all the way, worried for all of them, but especially for little
Stevie. Her hand felt for Eb's and he grasped it tightly,
sparing her a reassuring smile.

The minutes seemed like hours as they sped into town.
Eb had no sooner parked the vehicle in the parking lot
than Jessica was out the door, hurrying with Dallas right
beside her to guide her steps.

Eb and Sally followed the couple into the small toy
store, and there was Stevie, sitting on the floor, playing
with a mechanical elephant that walked and lifted its trunk
and trumpeted.

"It's Stevie," Dallas said huskily. "He's...fine!"

"Where? Stevie!" Jessica called brokenly, holding out
her arms.

"Hi, Mom!" Stevie exclaimed, leaving the toy to run
into her arms. "Gosh, I was scared, but the man taught
me how to play poker and gave me a soda! He said I was
brave and he admired my courage! Were you scared,
Mom?"

Jessica was crying so hard that she could barely speak
at all. She hugged her child close and couldn't seem to let
him go, even when he wiggled.

"Let his dad have a little of this joyful reunion," Dallas
murmured dryly, holding out his arms.

Stevie went right into them and hugged him hard. "I
don't have a real dad now," he said, "but you're going to
be a great dad, Dallas! You and me will go to all the

wrestling matches and take Mom and describe everything to her, won't we?"

"Yes," Dallas said, his voice husky, his eyes bright as he rocked his child in his arms with mingled relief and affection. "We'll do that."

Jessica felt her way into Dallas's arms with Stevie and pressed there for a long moment. Beside them, Sally held tight to Eb's hand and smiled with pure relief.

"I had an adventure," Stevie said when his parents let go of him. "But it's nice to be home again. Can I have that elephant? He sure is neat!"

"You can have a whole circus if I can find one for sale," Dallas laughed huskily. "But for now, I think we'll go back to the ranch."

They paid for the elephant and got into the truck with Eb and Sally.

"Can you drop us off at our house?" Jessica asked Eb. There was a hesitation. She heard it and smiled.

"Lopez said that he had no more business with me," Jessica told him. "He didn't even question what I told him," she added. "He said that Isabella was always asking him questions and pretending to care about him. He knew she didn't. He did sound very sorry that he killed her. Perhaps the small part of him that's still human can feel remorse. Who knows?"

"One day," Dallas said curtly, "we'll catch up with him. This isn't over, you know, even if he is through making threats toward you and Stevie. He's going to pay for this. And, somehow, we're going to stop him from setting up business in Jacobsville."

"We have Rodrigo in place," Eb agreed, "and Cy watching the progress of the warehouse. It won't be easy, but if we're careful, we may cut his source of supply and his distribution network right in half. Cut off the head and the snake dies.''

''Amen,'' Dallas replied.

Dallas got out of the sports utility vehicle with Jessica and Stevie, waving the other couple off with a big smile.

''You really believe Lopez meant it when he said he was quits with Jessica?'' Sally asked, still not quite convinced of the outlaw's sincerity.

''Yes, I do,'' Eb replied, glancing at her with a smile. ''He's a snake, but his word is worth something.''

Sally turned her head toward Eb and studied his profile warmly, with soft, covetous eyes.

He glanced over and met that look. His own eyes narrowed. ''A lot has happened since last night,'' he said quietly. ''Do you still mean what you told me at dawn?''

''That I'd marry you?'' she asked.

He nodded.

''Oh, yes,'' she said, ''I meant every word. I want to live with you all my life.''

''It won't bother you to have professional mercenaries running around the place at all hours for a while?'' he teased.

She grinned. ''Why should it? I am, after all, a mercenary's woman.''

''Not quite yet,'' he murmured with a wry glance. ''And very soon, a mercenary's wife.''

''That sounds very respectable,'' she commented.

''I'm glad you waited for me, Sally,'' he said seriously.

''So am I.'' She slid her hand into his big one and held on tight. It tingled all the way up her arm.

''We've had enough excitement for today,'' he said. ''But tomorrow we'll see about getting the license. Do you want a justice of the peace or a minister to marry us?''

"A minister," she said at once. "I want a permanent marriage."

He nodded. "So do I. And you have to have a white gown with a veil."

Her eyebrows arched.

"You're not just a mercenary's woman, you're a virtuous mercenary's woman. I want to watch you float down the aisle to me covered in silk and satin and lace, and with a veil for me to lift after we've said our vows."

She smiled with her whole heart. "That would be nice. There's a little boutique…"

"We'll fly up to Dallas and get one at Neiman-Marcus."

She gasped.

"You're marrying a rich man," he pointed out. "Humor me. It's going to be a social event. Let me deck you out like a comet."

She laughed. "All right. I'd really love a white wedding, if you don't mind."

"And we'll both wear rings," he added. "We'll get those in Dallas, too."

Her eyes were full of dreams as she looked at her future husband hungrily. There was only one small worry. "Eb, about Maggie…"

"Maggie is a closed chapter," he told her. "I adored her, in my way, but she was never in love with me. I stood in Cord's shadow even then, and she never realized it. She still hasn't." He glanced at her and smiled. "I love you, you know," he murmured, watching her eyes light up. "I'd never have proposed if I hadn't."

"I love you, too, Eb," she said solemnly. "I always will."

His fingers curled tighter into hers. "Dreams really do come true."

She wouldn't have argued with that statement to save her life, and she said so.

It was the society event of the year in Jacobsville, eclipsed only by Simon Hart's wedding with the governor giving Tira away. There were no major celebrities at Eb and Sally's wedding, but Eb did have a conglomeration of mercenaries and government agents the like of which Jacobsville had never seen. Cord Romero was sitting with Maggie on the groom's side of the church, along with a tall, striking dark-haired man with a small mustache and neat brief beard. Beside him was a big blond man who made even Dallas look shorter. On the pew across from him, on Sally's side of the church, was a blue-eyed brunette who avoided looking at the big blond man. Sally recognized her as Callie, the stepsister of the big blond man, who was Eb's friend Micah Steele.

A number of men in suits filled the rest of the groom's pews. Some were wearing sunglasses inside. Others were watching the people on the bride's side of the church, which wasn't packed, since Sally hadn't been back in Jacobsville long enough to make close friends in the community. Jessica was there with Stevie and Dallas, of course.

Sally walked down the aisle all by herself, since she hadn't contacted either of her parents about her wedding. They had their own lives now, and neither of them had written to Sally since the breakup of their family when she moved in with Jessica. She didn't really mind going it alone. Somehow, under the circumstances, it even seemed appropriate. She wore a dream of a wedding gown, with yards and yards of delicate lace and a train, and a veil that accentuated her blond beauty.

Eb stood at the altar waiting for her, in a gray vested

suit with a white rose in his lapel. He turned as she joined him, and looked down at her with eyes that made her knees weak.

The ceremony was brief, but poignant, and when Eb lifted the veil to kiss her for the first time as her husband, tears welled up in her eyes as his mouth tenderly claimed hers. They held hands going back down the aisle, wearing matching simple gold bands. Outside the church, they were pelted with rice and good wishes. Laughing, Sally tossed her bouquet and Dallas intercepted it to make sure it landed in Jessica's hands.

They climbed into the rented limousine and minutes later, they were at Eb's ranch, pausing just long enough to change into traveling clothes and rush to the private airstrip to board a loaned Learjet for the trip to Puerto Vallarta, Mexico, for their brief honeymoon.

The trip was tiring, and so was the aftermath of the day's excitement. Sally climbed into the huge whirlpool bath while Eb made dinner reservations for that evening.

She didn't realize that she wasn't alone until Eb climbed down into the water with her. He chuckled at her expression and then he kissed her. Very soon, she forgot all about her shock at the first sight of her unclothed bridegroom in the joy of an embrace that knew no obstacles.

He kissed her until she was clinging, gasping for breath and shivering with pleasure.

"Where?" he whispered, stroking her tenderly, enjoying her reactions to her first real intimacy. "Here, or in the bed?"

She could barely speak. "In bed," she said huskily.

"That suits me."

He got out and turned off the jets, lifting her clear of the water to towel them both dry. He picked her up and carried her quickly into the bedroom, barely taking time to strip down the covers before he fell with her onto crisp, clean sheets.

She knew that first times were notoriously painful, embarrassing, and uncomfortable, but hers was a notable exception. Eb was skillful and slow, arousing her to a hot frenzy of response before he even began to touch her intimately. By the time his body slid down against hers in stark possession, she was lifting toward him and pleading for an end to the violent tension of pleasure he'd aroused in her.

Her breath jerked out at his ear at the slow, steady invasion of her most private place in a silence that magnified the least little sound. She heard his heartbeat, and her own, increase with every careful thrust of his hips. She heard his breathing, erratic, rough, mingling with her own excited little moans.

She felt one lean hand sliding up her bare leg as he turned and shifted his weight against her, and when he touched her high on her inner thigh in a rhythm like the descent of his body, she arched up toward him and groaned in anguish.

He laughed softly at her temple while he increased the rhythm and caressed her in the most outrageous ways, all the while whispering things so shocking that she gasped. Tossed between waves of pleasure that grew with each passing second, she found herself suddenly suspended somewhere high above reality as she went over some intangible cliff and fell shuddering with ecstasy into a white-hot oblivion.

She felt him there with her, felt his pleasure in her body, felt his own release even as hers threatened to last forever. She wondered dimly if she was going to survive the incredible delight of it. She shivered helplessly as pleasure washed over her and she clung harder to the source of it, pleading for him not to stop.

When she was finally exhausted and barely able to catch her breath, he tucked her close in his arms and pulled the sheet over them.

"Sleep now," he whispered, kissing her forehead.

"Like this?" she asked unsteadily.

"Just like this." He wrapped her closer. "We'll sleep a little. And then..."

"And then."

The dinner reservations went unclaimed. Through the long night, she learned more than she'd ever dreamed about men and bodies and lovemaking. For a first time, she told her delighted husband, it was quite extraordinary.

They had breakfast in bed and then set out to explore the old city. But by evening, they were exploring each other again.

A week later, they arrived back home at Eb's ranch, to find a flurry of new activity. A local undercover DEA agent, whose wife Lisa Monroe lived on a ranch next door to Cy Parks, had been found murdered. Apparently he'd infiltrated Lopez's organization and been discovered. Rodrigo was still undercover, and Eb was concerned for him. The warehouse next door to Cy was in the final stages of construction. Things were heating up in Jacobsville.

"At least we had a honeymoon," Eb murmured dryly, hugging his new wife close.

"So we did," she agreed. She looked up at him lovingly. "And now you're back off adventuring."

"Well, so are you," he pointed out. "After all, isn't teaching second-graders a daily adventure as well?"

She hugged him close. "Being married to you is the

biggest adventure, but you have to promise not to ever get shot at again."

"I give you my word as a Girl Scout," he murmured dryly.

She punched him in the stomach. "And if you wade into battle, I'll be right there beside you holding spare cartridges."

He searched her eyes. "You really are a hell of a woman," he murmured.

She grinned. "I'm glad you noticed."

"Lucky me," he said only half facetiously, and bent to kiss her with unbridled passion. "Lucky, lucky me!" he added while he could manage speech.

Sally wrapped her arms around him and held on tight, as intoxicated with pleasure as he was. There would always be the threat of danger, but nothing that the mercenary and his woman couldn't handle. But for the moment, she had her soldier of fortune right where she wanted him—in her gentle, loving arms.

In January 2001
Silhouette Desire
presents the next book in
Diana Palmer's provocative new
Soldiers of Fortune *trilogy:*

THE WINTER SOLDIER

*Cy Parks had a reputation around Jacobsville
for being meaner than a rattlesnake. But Lisa
Monroe wasn't afraid of the mesmerizing
mercenary and drove him to distraction with
her tantalizing kisses. Though he'd never admit
it, Cy was getting mighty possessive of the
pregnant, practically penniless widow who
needed the type of safeguarding only he could
provide. But who would protect the beguiling
beauty from him?*

Soldiers of Fortune...prisoners of love.

*Turn the page for an exciting sneak
preview of Silhoutte Desire's unforgettable
Man of the Month...*

Cy Parks had his first good night's sleep in days. He'd sent a capable, older cowboy over to Lisa Monroe's neighboring ranch the night before to sleep in the bunkhouse and keep an eye on things. He'd also arranged covertly for sensitive listening equipment to be placed around her house, and for a man to monitor it full-time. He might be overly cautious, but he wasn't taking chances with a pregnant woman. He knew Manuel Lopez's thirst for revenge far too well. The drug lord had a nasty habit of targeting the families of people who opposed him. Cy wasn't willing to risk leaving Lisa out there alone.

Her situation was precarious. Pregnant, widowed and deeply in debt, she was likely to find herself homeless before much longer, when the bank was forced to foreclose on the small ranch her father had left her as a legacy. Lisa's husband, an undercover narcotics officer with a federal agency, had recently been killed by Lopez's men when he tried to infiltrate the drug lord's organization. He had borrowed on his life insurance policy, so there had been just enough money to bury him.

The next day Cy drove over to Lisa's house and found her struggling with a cow in the barn, trying to pull a calf by hand. He couldn't believe she was actually doing that!

He'd barely cut off the engine before he was out of the big sports utility vehicle and towering over her in the barn. She looked up with a grimace on her face when she realized what a temper he was in.

"Don't you say a word, Cy Parks," she said at once, wiping the sweat from her forehead. "There's nobody but me to do this, and the cow can't wait until one of my part-timers comes in from the lower pasture. They're dipping cattle…"

"So you're trying to do a job that you aren't half big enough to manage. Are you out of your mind?" he burst out. "You're pregnant, for God's sake!"

"Barely two weeks pregnant." She was panting, sprawled between the cow's legs. She glared up at him and blew a stray strand of hair out of her sweaty eyes. "Listen, I can't afford to lose the cow or the calf…"

"Get up!" he said harshly.

She glared at him.

For all the raging temper in his eyes, he reached down and lifted her tenderly to her feet, putting her firmly to one side. Cy studied her openly. She was sweet, but she wouldn't win any beauty contests. Her dark blond hair was always in a bun and she never wore makeup. She wore glasses over her brown eyes, plastic framed ones, and her usual garb was jeans and a T-shirt when she was working around the ranch. He got down on one knee beside the cow and looked at the situation grimly. "Have you got a calf-pull?"

She ground her teeth together. "No. It broke and I didn't know how to fix it."

He said a few words under his breath and went out to his truck, using the radio to call for help. Fortunately one of his men was barely two minutes away. Harley, his foreman, came roaring up beside Cy's truck, braked and jumped out with a length of rope.

"Good man, Harley," Cy said as he looped the calf's feet. "If we can't get him out ourselves, we can use the wrench on my truck. Ready? Pull!"

They were bathed in sweat and cursing by the time they managed to pull the calf out. Cy cleared his nose and mouth and the little black-baldy bawled. The cow turned, gently licking her calf.

"That was a near miss," Harley observed, grinning.

"Very near." Cy glowered at Lisa. "In more ways than one."

"Excuse me?" Harley asked.

"It was my cow," Lisa pointed out. "I thought I could do it by myself."

"Pregnant, and you think you're Samson," he said with biting sarcasm.

She put her hands on her hips and glare up at him. "Go away!"

"Gladly. When I've washed my hands," Cy muttered, glancing at his stitched arm. It had been injured from an encounter with one of his angry Santa Gertrudis bulls. It was his left arm, too, the one that had been burned in the house fire back in Wyoming. "I've got a raw wound. I'll have to have antibacterial soap."

"Antibacterial soap, indeed. The germs would probably die of natural causes if they got you!" Lisa muttered.

"At least my germs are intelligent! I wouldn't try pulling calves if I was pregnant!"

Lisa almost doubled over at the thought of a pregnant Cy Parks.

His bad mood subsided at the sight of Lisa's dark eyes bubbling with joy. Her laughter was infectious. She made him hungry, thirsty, desperate for the delight she awakened in him....

If you enjoyed what you just read,
then we've got an offer you can't resist!

Take 2 bestselling love stories FREE!

Plus get a FREE surprise gift!

Look Who's Celebrating Our 20th Anniversary:

Celebrate
20
YEARS

"Happy 20th birthday, Silhouette. You made the writing dream of hundreds of women a reality. You enabled us to give [women] the stories [they] wanted to read and helped us teach [them] about the power of love."

—*New York Times* bestselling author
Debbie Macomber

"I wish you continued success, Silhouette Books.... Thank you for giving me a chance to do what I love best in all the world."

—International bestselling author
Diana Palmer

"A visit to Silhouette is a guaranteed happy ending, a chance to touch magic for a little while.... It refreshes and revitalizes and makes us feel better.... I hope Silhouette goes on forever."

—Award-winning bestselling author
Marie Ferrarella

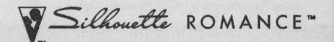

Silhouette ROMANCE™